THE FISHING CREEK
CONFEDERACY

THE FISHING CREEK
CONFEDERACY

BYRON HELLER

iUniverse, Inc.
Bloomington

THE FISHING CREEK CONFEDERACY

iUniverse books may be ordered through booksellers or by contacting:

iUniverse
1663 Liberty Drive
Bloomington, IN 47403
www.iuniverse.com
1-800-Authors (1-800-288-4677)

Because of the dynamic nature of the Internet, any web addresses or links contained in this book may have changed since publication and may no longer be valid. The views expressed in this work are solely those of the author and do not necessarily reflect the views of the publisher, and the publisher hereby disclaims any responsibility for them.

Any people depicted in stock imagery provided by Thinkstock are models, and such images are being used for illustrative purposes only.
Certain stock imagery © Thinkstock.

ISBN: 978-1-4759-5665-8 (sc)
ISBN: 978-1-4759-5666-5 (ebk)

Library of Congress Control Number: 2012919644

Printed in the United States of America

iUniverse rev. date: 11/14/2012

To Peter + Sydney:

I hope you enjoy this little tale from my neck of the woods. There is also a non-fictional book by the same name.

Byron

INTRODUCTION

S ome movie previews herald films that have been in
production for years. One might say this book has been
decades in the making. It began in 1968, when I was a student
at Bloomsburg State College (now Bloomsburg University).
The name of the political science class has been lost in the fog
of time, but it was taught by James Percey. Each student was
to write a paper. For reasons I no longer remember, I chose
the topic "Presidential Voting History of Columbia County,
Pennsylvania."

In the process of researching the paper, I came across the
curious topic of the Fishing Creek Confederacy, also known
as the Invasion of Columbia County. A few years later in
1972, after accepting a job offer I couldn't refuse from Uncle
Sam, I found myself at the University of Maryland graduate
school. One of the instructors in the Government and Politics
Department, Dr. Franklin L. Burdette, had a down-home
folksy approach to teaching political science. He too required
a paper, and I remembered the Fishing Creek Confederacy.
Dr. Burdette was receptive to the original fifty-six-page paper.
I decided that if I ever retired, I would dig out the paper and
expand on it.

About once a decade I would come across the paper, and
in 2006, I retired. So it was back to Bloomsburg University, the
Columbia County Historical Society, and Bucknell University.
Three of the main characters, Senator Charles Buckalew,

General George Cadwalader, and Colonel John Freeze were real persons. Jacob Saddler, Katherine Winder, and Lieutenant Michael Kelly are fictional. Their interaction can tell us much about the thinking of many people at that time.

The entire episode is but a small part of the Civil War and is little known outside the local community. Similar stories were played out in other parts of the North as civilians were arrested and held in several military installations. Some readers may be offended by some of the language. However, to rephrase various words and phrases in modern parlance would be inaccurate and would fail to convey the ferocity of the sentiments in play at the time.

I realize that some historical purists object to historical fiction. One of my hobbies is Irish history. I love Irish folk music and, for a long time, hated Irish folk music turned into rock music. However, the younger generation responded to Irish rock music, and I realized that perhaps this was the key to getting some of the young people to begin thinking about the people and events revealed in the music. I now view historical fiction in somewhat the same way. It is not pure history, but if by spinning a more interesting tale one might get the younger generation to begin asking questions about the topic and perhaps begin their own research, it is well worth the effort.

Where do I stand in the battle between the protagonists in this little tale? I say a pox upon both your houses. The Democrats should have supported the war to save the Union and, perhaps even more importantly, to free their fellow humans from bondage. As for the Republicans, they took the opportunity to trample the civil liberties of their local opponents and clearly held unlawful trials of several defendants. Criticism may be tempered somewhat by judging both sides using the morals and lack of understanding of the time. Yet I feel there are certain minimal standards that one must adhere to, such as freedom from slavery and the right to free speech. The first standard is absolute. As for free speech, the boundaries are not yet set in stone and may be argued for generations to come.

Acknowledgments

B ecause this book has been so long in the works, there are most likely many people along the road who have assisted me but whom I have forgotten. However, I will recognize those I can remember.

I must first thank my wife, Suzanne, who provided invaluable assistance in typing and retyping page after page, including the redraft of an entire chapter. I may have been able to hunt and peck my way through this book, but Suzanne did a much more efficient job and made corrections and suggestions along the way.

A thank you must go to Bill Blando. That would have read "my very good friend Bill Blando," but I am ever aware of his admonition to "keep it short." Bill is a retired newspaperman who graciously volunteered to proofread this manuscript. There have been numerous corrections and changes. Being the gentleman he is, he continued with his assistance, even through the adversity of losing his wife, Betty. It can be truthfully said that this book would not have been presentable to the public had it not been for Bill's tireless efforts.

The rest of the acknowledgments will follow in rough chronological order. When I began my research in 1972, Mr. Edwin Barton of the Columbia County Historical Society was most helpful in guiding me to sources and encouraging me with my project.

The staff members at the Bloomsburg State College (now Bloomsburg University) were very helpful as were the people at the Bloomsburg Morning Press. Dr. Franklin Burdette of the University of Maryland liked the early version and encouraged me to expand upon it.

More recently, Mr. Robert Dunkelberger of Bloomsburg University was kind enough to open the archives section to me on two occasions. He too took time to speak to me about my project. The staff at the library was helpful in assisting me with finding sources filed in their computers.

The current staff at the Columbia County Historical Society opened their records and was helpful in suggesting sources. While researching there, I had the pleasure of speaking with Dr. George A. Turner of Bloomsburg University. Dr. Turner is an expert on the Fishing Creek Confederacy. He was kind enough to take an hour of his time to speak with me. His knowledge on the subject was so enthralling that I forgot about the time, leading to a parking ticket. The fine was well worth it.

Lastly, I must thank the staff at the Bucknell Library for their assistance. The Pennsylvania section included a few sources not available at Bloomsburg.

THE FISHING CREEK
CONFEDERACY

This is a story of resistance to the Civil War in Columbia County, Pennsylvania, and the government's response.

Chapter I

APPREHENSION

Jacob slept a deep and peaceful sleep. It was a sleep born only from the merger of a hard day's work and a clear conscience. He did not hear the distant sergeant barking orders to his blue-clad troops. Perhaps it was best.

Across the room, close, but not too close to the hearth, lay Toby. Nine years before, Jacob's mother had died. The boy was inconsolable. In hopes of lifting his depression, his father presented him with Toby. Of course, no mere puppy could ever replace a boy's mother. However, Jacob and Toby would form that bond known only to a boy and his dog. In his younger years, Toby would run down rabbits, squirrels, and other animals. Groundhogs were not much of a challenge but often gave a pretty good fight. In recent years, he had noticed that the animals ran faster. Perhaps, this was proof of Mr. Darwin's newfangled theories on animal evolution. Toby's sleep also was deep but fitful. In his sleep, he was young again and able to chase down his prey. His chase resulted in foot spasms and occasional yips. He did not hear the rumble of canteens on leather belts or the rattle of bayonets on rifle barrels. Perhaps it was best.

Neither the boy nor dog heard the muffled whispers outside or the stealing of boots across the wooden porch. Suddenly, the sergeant's boot rammed the front door. The top of the door was blasted away from the upper hinge, and the latch was shattered into dozens of wooden shards. In an instant, the room was filled with angry voices. "Traitor! Copperhead! Rebel!" Toby was immediately on the defensive, barking and growling. Jacob sat bolt upright in his bed. Surely, this must be a dream. No, no, he could feel the morning air on his face and the cool of the floorboards on his feet. He made an attempt to get up and engage the men in conversation. He took no more than a few steps when a rifle butt ripped into his sternum. Jacob stumbled backward, falling over his bed and hitting his shoulders and head on the wall. He was in a daze and, for a short time, could not breathe. He was jolted from this condition by a shrill yelp. Looking across the room, he saw Toby suspended in midair, his small paws fighting mightily but vainly for traction. Suddenly, his body went limp. Slowly, Toby began to move forward in midair. Then with increasing velocity, he was hurled backward off the point of the bayonet. His small body smashed into the wall and slithered to the floor, leaving a crimson trail behind. "No!" shouted Jacob. He sprang forward, attempting to assist his friend. He made it no more than a few steps before he was tripped and slammed to the floor. In an instant, he forgot about Toby as he was pummeled by boots and rifle butts. He instinctively curled up to protect himself. It seemed like an eternity before the beating ceased.

Jacob was yanked to his feet, and his nightshirt was ripped off of him. He stood there in only his long johns. His face reddened, and he became embarrassed as the men poked fun at him. In a short time, his cotton shirt was thrown in his face. He fumbled with the buttons and turned away from the men. He did not want them to see how nervous he was or that his fingers would not work. He was then thrown his woolen pants. The buttons on the shirt had presented quite a problem. The buttons on the coarse woolen pants were even worse. When he finished this task, it was an easy matter to move the suspenders over his shoulders. Next, he was allowed to put on his shoes and socks.

He was then forced forward to the door. A corporal's boot made quick work of the lower portion of the door, flattening it on the front porch. Before he left, Jacob looked to his right. The pool of blood surrounding Toby had stopped expanding. The poor dog's eyes had just begun to glaze over. However, the most gruesome aspect was the grotesque way in which the dog's tongue hung from his mouth. Jacob vowed that he would remember this scene forever.

Once outside, the morning breeze brushed his face and helped awaken him. Four soldiers were placed to his right and four to his left. There were two behind him with the sergeant in front. The sergeant looked at him, saying, "I am no good on legal talk. You are arrested for interfering with the war effort and the draft. Boy, if it were up to me, we'd simply take a rope and throw it over that tree. Then we'd see if you could do a little dance for us. However, I'm duty-bound to bring you in. You may be thinking about running. If you do, remember there are nine of us and only one of you. Even if you're lucky enough to outrun us, I guarantee you won't outrun the Minie-balls. Do you understand me, boy?"

Jacob nodded that he did.

The small band headed left around the cornfield. Before leaving, Jacob stole a last look at his small home. He wondered for the first time if he would ever see it again. The group made it down the buggy-rutted lane to the dirt road. They turned left onto the dirt road leading to Benton. In a short time, the sun had burned off the morning dew, and the road became dusty. Clouds of dust, like shrouds in the wind, surrounded the soldiers and Jacob. Some of the soldiers put kerchiefs around their noses, and some simply cursed the dust. All of them began coughing. However, Jacob welcomed the dust. The soldiers were tearing up because of the dust. Who was to say that Jacob was not also tearing up from the dust rather than from fear and humiliation? He also was glad to be able to cough because he could use that to stifle his sobs. For the first time, he understood the term "lump in the throat." It had felt as though someone had placed a large stone beneath his sternum. He had difficulty breathing and began to panic. He realized that panicking and trying to run would mean sure death. He forced his mind to think of other things.

He went back in time. His earliest memory was of sitting on the front porch with his mother who sat in a rocking chair. She was husking corn. Jacob's job was to assist her by removing the silken hairs. At other times, he would help remove the pods from peas or snap beans.

He remembered his mother as being tall and strong. Despite her muscular build, she had a thin waist. Her hair was chestnut colored and her eyes were gray-green. Once a week the family would get in the buggy and go to meeting at Millville, about an eleven-mile journey. In the wintertime they used the sleigh. Jacob could remember his mother heating bricks on the hearth. They were transferred to a perforated tin box and from hence to the sleigh to be used as a foot warmer.

She was a good Quaker, except for one thing. She loved to dance. In Philadelphia, it was difficult to attend a dance without being spotted. However, in Columbia County she had her choice of barn dances nearly every weekend. Jacob's father was a reluctant partner in the square dances but refused to engage in waltzes or similar dances. As for Jacob, he was content to sit in a corner with some punch and cheese and watch dancers all dressed in their finest clothes.

He also remembered his father and the day his father was chopping wood. Jacob was busy stacking the wood when it occurred to him that he had the harder job. He asked his father if he could split the wood. The father, with a bemused smile on his face, handed the maul to Jacob. Jacob took a swing at the oaken log. The log did not move. Jacob took another swing and managed to fray a small sliver of wood about the size of a toothpick. Sheepishly, he handed the maul back to his father and went back to stacking wood.

His best memories were of sitting with his mother and father before the fire in their small cabin. His father would be busy whittling objects or repairing small farm implements. His mother would be busy sewing, knitting, or mending garments. Occasionally, his father would read to them from the Good Book. However, his fondest remembrances were of stories of his ancestors.

He remembered his father telling him that his great-great-great-grandfather, Johann Saddler, had emigrated from Germany in 1751. The name of the town had been lost over time. However, family lore noted that Johann and his son, Peter, traveled north on the Rhine to Rotterdam. Previous émigrés had not realized that taxes were levied by small principalities along the Rhine. Thus, they arrived in Rotterdam without funds and often had to sell themselves as indentured servants to a ship's captain who would sell the indentures upon reaching the New World. Forewarned by the failures of prior emigrants, Johann Saddler had secured enough money for the trip and the taxes. Johann and Peter arrived in Philadelphia in September 1751.

Upon arrival, Johann had to take an oath of allegiance to King George III. The procedure for administering oaths was similar in England and Germany. Therefore, he knew that he was taking an oath and it had something to do with George III. The exact nature of the oath was lost on Johann, as the German who had been hired to administer the oath was from

Northern Germany and spoke in an unfamiliar dialect. Peter, being only six years old, did not have to take the oath. Johann moved to the area around York and secured work as a tailor. He soon earned enough money to have his wife, Eva, come over from Germany. Upon reaching age twelve, Peter obtained work as an apprentice for a tobacconist. After a few years, the family had saved enough money, and they bought a small farm outside of Benton, Pennsylvania. At the outbreak of the revolution, Peter was thirty-one years old.

He was recruited by the Committee of Safety and joined the colonial army. The committee had sent riders to the valley in hopes of filling the ranks. They succeeded beyond their dreams. There was no shortage of Scotch-Irish, Irish, or Germans ready to take up arms against the crown. The Scotch-Irish were still angered at being evicted from their ancestral homes. The Germans had been mocked by the English for their strange customs and guttural language. More than one German family had complaints of being cheated by the English in land deals. The Irish harbored an ancient hatred from the long occupation of their land by Crown forces. The Penal Laws had attempted to eradicate their culture and religion, restricted land ownership, and denied the right to engage in many skilled occupations. Then there were the tithes the Dissenters and Catholics were forced to pay in order to support the Church of Ireland.

For Peter, the question was not so much taxation without representation. He was quite literate and knew that the Founding Fathers had rejected representation in the British Parliament as noted in the Declaration and Resolves of the First Continental Congress. He, like many others, felt that any colonial representation in London would be swallowed up by British interests. The colonies had their own problems that were known to and solvable only by colonial legislatures.

Although some of the British taxes were meant to recoup money spent defending the colonies during the French and Indian War, other acts were seen as unjust. Primary among them was the Declaratory Act that reaffirmed Parliament's right to directly govern the colonies. Many people were willing to accept King George as their liege, but they were not willing to bow to the demands of a foreign legislature.

Peter was fortunate in that he did not have to see combat. Rather, he was assigned a job guarding Hessian prisoners. This was the perfect job for him, as he not only spoke the language but also the dialect. Although most of the prisoners were from Northern Hesse, the difference in dialect was not all that troubling. At times, the prisoners had to be moved due to the fortunes of war. The officers were paroled to the local area upon their promise not to escape. To a man, they kept their word.

Jacob especially liked the stories about his great-great-grandfather turning a blind eye while some of the young conscripted lads would "escape." The strapping young men from Hesse were in demand for farmwork. As such, they would "escape" with some slabs of meat wrapped in paper and, if fortunate, one or two pieces of fruit. They would often have a canteen of water and a short letter of introduction to the community, written auf Deutsch.

These escapees hoped to end up in remote areas seldom visited by British or mercenary troops. Given the number of men in the colonial militias, finding employment was no problem. Many ended up working on farms, just as they would have in Hesse. With luck, they would be able to save some money, marry a girl of German extraction, and move west to begin their own farms and families. Some of the men became enamored with the local Irish girls who seemed less taciturn than their German counterparts. Although there might be some language problems, there were no social taboos in a German-Irish wedding. What was still forbidden was crossing the Protestant-Catholic barrier.

While Peter was away serving in the military, the Great Runaway of the summer of 1778 occurred. At that point, a force of British regulars, Tories, and Indians attacked the West Branch Valley. Only three hundred American militiamen defended this area. Over three thousand settlers fled their homes. The Saddler family was ready to flee when the invading force withdrew. When his enlistment was up, Peter returned to his family and farm.

After farming for a year or so, Peter felt that the threat had abated and that his children were old enough to take on the increasing burdens of running the farm. Therefore, he reenlisted. This time, he was assigned to an elite group of Pennsylvanian riflemen. One day, they were ordered to ambush a group of British sentries.

Unfortunately, his band attacked the sentries at the changing of the guard, and they met a force twice the expected size. The purpose of the attack was not so much to kill Redcoats but to take prisoners. The attack succeeded, and his party returned with a large number of prisoners. The British officer refused to answer any questions involving the military. Peter considered the British to be a vain lot. Being an enlisted man, he was not allowed to interrogate an officer. So he suggested a strategy to those who would interrogate the British captain. Basically, the captain was told that as he was a low-ranking officer of little importance, he could not have any valuable information. Accordingly, his interrogation would be brief. The British officer was highly offended. He was important—he had information and he would let the colonials know it. It was only later he realized that he had, in effect, been outwitted by a mere private.

Peter's son, Mathias, was now thirteen years old. In his father's absence, he became the man of the family. In October 1780, Indians invaded the valley of Fishing Creek and attacked the Van Campen family. The Saddlers, along with others, fled to Fort Wheeler at Lightstreet. Fort Wheeler was not really a fort but basically a stockade of sharpened stakes placed around the farmhouse of Isaiah Wheeler. That farmhouse was one of the largest and sturdiest in the area. A killing zone of three hundred yards was cleared around the stockade. At that range, Pennsylvania rifles were relatively accurate while the muskets used by the British and Indians were not. Therefore, any British soldier or Indian walking into the clearing was fair game.

Mathias proved to be adept at using his father's old musket. Thus, he was given a new Pennsylvania rifle to shoot. Although the Pennsylvania rifle was accurate, it was nearly five feet long and had a slender stock. Therefore, it tended to be end-heavy. Although not yet fourteen years old, Mathias was nearly six feet tall and weighed 190 pounds, enabling him to hold the rifle as steady as any grown man. And he could hit a human-size figure at three hundred yards. More amazingly, he was able to hit a twig at forty yards. As such, he was given the Pennsylvania rifle in exchange for his defense of the fort. When the fort was attacked, his fire proved deadly to his enemies. Prior to a second attack, the defenders of the fort ran low on ammunition and powder. It was determined that two runners should be sent to Fort Jenkins for powder and lead. Mathias was not the fastest runner in the fort, but he had great endurance. Although they hated to lose their best marksman, he would be of no use if the fort ran out of powder and ammunition. Mathias and another runner were dispatched to Fort Jenkins and shortly returned with sufficient powder and lead. The fort held out and, indeed, was the only fort in the area that was never taken by the British.

Jacob had always loved hearing this part of the family history. His mother was a member of the Society of Friends and was less enthusiastic about such stories. However, in her infinite patience, she managed to abide the retelling of the story, reminding herself that it was part of the family's history.

Later, Mathias Saddler was to marry Katrina Baumgardner. In 1795, they had their first child, George Worthington Saddler. George was to fight in the Battle of Baltimore during the War of 1812. He often said that the British suffered as much from the Maryland heat and their wool coats as they did from the marksmanship of the militia. In 1818, George married. Being a Lutheran family, they named their second son Melancthon after Luther's assistant.

Melancthon was Jacob's father. During the summer of 1838, Melancthon met Ellen Whittaker. She was a young Quaker girl who was visiting relatives in the area. Her family had a history of being Philadelphia merchants. The two fell in love. Initially, neither family approved of the match. George was not happy that his son was enamored with a Quaker, not to mention one of English background. On the other hand, the Whittakers were unhappy that their daughter had fallen in love with this farmer from the outback who had no promising prospects. However, the Whittakers finally determined that Ellen was moved by her inner feelings and that the match could not be denied. In exchange for her moving to the hinterlands, Melancthon converted to her religion.

Ellen had never been comfortable in the Philadelphia setting. Basically, things moved too quickly, and she felt that many people were insincere. She was fond of saying that the Quakers were a religious group that had "come to America to do good and had done well." The farmwork was harder than that to which she had been accustomed, but she found the peacefulness of a rural setting much to her satisfaction. Although Jacob was to be born in 1846 without incident, Ellen was to suffer a number of miscarriages. In 1855, she carried her infant daughter to term. Unfortunately, there were complications during delivery, and Ellen died. The little girl was born with mucus in her respiratory system. She died at birth.

It was at this point that Jacob became depressed, and his father gave him Toby. He remembered how helpless Toby was at first. The small dog had difficulty climbing the ridges and fell into the furrows in an attempt to run to his master and new friend who was plowing the fields. However, within a few weeks, the dog was bounding around and chasing everything in sight. Toby also accompanied Jacob to school. Although Toby was not allowed in the school, he amused himself by playing outside. During the winter months, he dug a hole outside the school wall nearest the Franklin stove, gaining some warmth.

The schoolteacher in the one-room school was Miss Agatha Mayes, with the emphasis on "Miss." Her contract, as with most at the time, required that she resign her position should she marry. Pregnancy was a basis for immediate dismissal. The dichotomy was that male teachers were expected to marry, raise a family, and continue teaching. The fact they were expected to support a family was used as an excuse to pay male teachers more than their female counterparts.

Jacob also remembered that terrible day almost two years ago, when his father was cutting a tree near the creek bank. The stone on which he was standing slipped, and the ax came down on his left ankle. Jacob hooked up the horse and buggy as fast as he could. He helped Malancthon onto the back of the buggy but noted that he was very pale. By the time he reached the nearest doctor, his father had lost too much blood. Jacob became an orphan at the age of sixteen.

Now Jacob was responsible for running the farm on his own. Like his father, he attended markets in Benton and other nearby towns to sell his produce. On one such adventure, he met Katherine Winder. Her father, Harry Winder, was a local merchant. He had started out as a blacksmith and had saved enough money to buy a coal yard. He then rented the blacksmith shop to his apprentice. Between the profits from the blacksmith shop and coal yard, he was able to purchase a small dry-goods store. He was one of the more successful merchants in the area and was a leading figure in the Republican Party. As such, he was a big backer of the Lincoln administration and the Civil War. Understandably, he was not pleased by the thought that his daughter had fallen in love with a mere farmer, not to mention a Quaker. That summer, Jacob and Katherine would take walks in Benton and sometimes go into the woods on picnics. They often flirted, but they also spoke of the war. Katherine accepted her father's assertion that the war was necessary. Jacob held to his Quaker beliefs. Although slavery was an evil institution, the problem could be resolved by discussion. After all, at one point every state had allowed slavery in some form. The Northern states had seen the light and had abolished slavery without violence. Surely, Southerners could be persuaded to do the same.

Courtship for Katherine and Jacob fell into four categories. There were church picnics with other couples, chaperoned by the parson and his wife. The couple was allowed to meet in the Winder parlor or front porch with either Mister or Missus Winder nearby. There were walks around town with Mrs. Winder following and twirling her parasol. She kept far enough behind to permit private conversation, but near enough to prohibit any inappropriate touching. Lastly, there were social functions, such as dances and fairs.

Jacob had taken two steps before he realized that his captors had stopped marching. Rather sheepishly, he stopped and took two steps backward. He looked around and noticed another group of soldiers with three additional prisoners. They were all sitting at an intersection under a large elm tree. His group joined them, and he was placed with the other three prisoners. One of them was a local man whom he knew rather well. The second was only vaguely familiar, as Jacob had seen him at a meeting of the Patrons of Husbandry. The third man was a stranger.

By dribs and drabs, additional troops and new prisoners converged at the Benton Church. Inside the church, a Union captain held sway on the pulpit. Beside him was an informer who often whispered in the captain's ear. By the time the troops were done, nearly one hundred men had been apprehended. Each was quickly taken before the captain, and a snap decision was made as to whether the person would be released or remanded. Jacob, like many of the others, was unaware of the specific charges or activities that had brought him to this end. Unfortunately for Jacob, he was held over with forty-four other prisoners. They were placed in a nineteen-by-forty-three-foot holding pen and were fed by the family of John Stiles, one of the prisoners. The captain had concluded his work by late morning, and forty-five prisoners were marched nearly eighteen miles south to Bloomsburg. Along the way, Jacob listened intently to the prisoners and any conversations he could pick up from the guards. The information he garnered was contradictory. Some guards indicated they were going to Harrisburg while others said their destination would be Philadelphia. Jacob felt they would most likely be taken to

Harrisburg, as that was the state capital and the likely venue for any trials. Upon reaching Bloomsburg, the prisoners were ordered into two waiting boxcars. The train soon pulled out, heading in a southeasterly direction. Jacob did not know his fate or his destination. The only certainty was that his future was uncertain.

Chapter II

ONSET OF CIVIL WAR

During the early eighteenth century, settlers began filtering out of Philadelphia into the fertile plains of Berks, Lycoming, and York counties. At the same time, settlers began moving west from settlements along the Delaware River. Many of these settlers ended up in valleys with streams flowing into the Susquehanna River. Although there are several streams in Pennsylvania called Fishing Creek, our attention is centered upon the one in Columbia County. It arises at North Mountain and flows east before turning south. Near the town of Forks, it merges with Huntingdon Creek and continues down to empty into the Susquehanna River near the town of Rupert.

Many of these settlers, or their parents, fled their European communities because of religious intolerance, military conscription, or economic hardship. To a man, they were highly independent and suspicious of anything having to do with government. Many would have subscribed to the adage "That government is best which governs least." As such, many were anti-federalists and later Democrats.

By the mid-nineteenth century, the residents of Columbia County, like their counterparts throughout the nation, argued over the issue of slavery. The opinions in the county, reflecting that of the nation, ran a wide gamut from those who believed that slavery was a fact of life as indicated by history to those who demanded immediate abolition. To the former, it was clear that the Greek, Romans, Egyptians, and many European tribes had held slaves. It was apparent to them that this was simply a matter of a superior people dominating inferior people. On the other hand, there were those who believed in abolitionism and millennialism. Basically, they viewed slavery as an abomination. They believed that the time of troubles revealed in the book of Revelation was near. They felt it was the duty of every Christian to prepare for the second coming of the Messiah by liberating humanity from all political and social ills; foremost among these was the institution of slavery. To them, the elimination of slavery was not only a political and moral issue but a religious necessity.

It would be no overstatement to say that the election of 1860 was the most divisive in American history. After all, it was the only election that resulted in war. On the national level, Abraham Lincoln, the Republican candidate, took a plurality of votes. He obtained 39.8 percent of the vote with Senator Stephen Douglas, the Northern Democratic candidate, second at 29.5 percent of the vote. John Breckenridge, the Southern Democratic candidate from Kentucky, tallied 18.1 percent, with John Bell, the Constitutional Union candidate from Tennessee, coming in fourth at 12.6 percent. Within the Commonwealth, Lincoln pulled 56.3 percent of the vote with Breckenridge second at 37.5 percent. Douglas and Bell trailed badly.

However, in Columbia County, Breckenridge, the pro-slavery candidate won the day, taking 2,367 votes to Lincoln's 1,873 votes. Douglas had eighty-six votes with Bell a poor fourth with only fourteen votes. In Benton, Orange, Fishing Creek, Jackson, and Sugarloaf townships, Breckenridge garnered 76 percent of the votes. The county held true to its Democrat traditions.

The election was held on November 6, 1860. On December 21, 1860, South Carolina seceded from the Union. This led to the firing on Fort Sumter on April 12, 1861, and the outbreak of the American Civil War.

The initial reaction of the county was one of outrage. Men flocked in droves to defend the Union. Squads grew into platoons, which in turn grew into companies. The companies became battalions that merged into regiments. The regiments filled up brigades and became divisions.

One of the first locals to volunteer was William Ricketts, a twenty-four-year-old from Orangeville. He had spent two years at West Point and had enrolled in Pennsylvania Medical College. He helped form the Iron Guards, which included twenty-seven men from Catawissa and nineteen from Bloomsburg. With a total of seventy-seven men, it formed one of ten companies comprising the Thirty-Fifth Regiment, Sixth Reserves of Pennsylvania Volunteers. They became part of the Army of the Potomac, and their first engagement was in December 1861 at Drainesville, Virginia, under Brigadier General George A. McCall, during which several hundred rebels were routed. The first local man to die in battle was Private Samuel C. Walter from Catawissa, a carpenter. The Iron Guards served under Generals George McClellan, John Pope, Ambrose Burnside, George Meade, and Ulysses Grant and were to fight in the battles of Richmond, Bull Run, Fredericksburg, Gettysburg, Bristoe Station, the Wilderness, Spotsylvania, and many more.

Colonel John Freeze, who wrote about the Fishing Creek Confederacy, was a member of the 112th Regiment, Second Artillery. He saw action in the Battle of the Wilderness, Petersburg, and Cold Harbor. In all, 1,447 men from Columbia County served in the military during the war, with 821 being drafted.

Although Ricketts was promoted from captain to colonel, he did not make it through the war. He became ill a few months after joining the army and resigned his commission on July 1, 1862. On August 10 of that year, he died of typhoid.

As with most wars, the initial mood was one of optimism. More than two thousand folks showed up to give the troops a hearty send-off. Barrels had planks nailed across them to form a speaker's platform. Handrails and steps were attached to provide access. Red, white, and blue bunting was attached to the rails and fluttered in the breeze. This was set up at the main square in Bloomsburg, up the hill from the fairgrounds and down the hill from the normal school. Nearly as far as one could see, horses were tethered to hitching posts. A parade was held, and a fife and drum corps assembled next to the speaker's platform in the northwest corner of the square. It was a fine day and gave the local volunteers a chance to show off their uniforms and newly learned marching skills for the young ladies. Vendors hawked candies, American flags, and various beverages.

One of the first speakers was the Reverend John Hess. He said, "Neighbors and fellow Christians, we are gathered here today to thank God for the brave men who are about to embark on a noble campaign. They have volunteered to save our homes and to defend the Union. There are some who would say that the Bible forbids Christians to engage in war. However, it is apparent that the Lord God Jehovah approved of the Israelites engaging in battle. The Old Testament is replete with stories of the Hebrews engaging in war.

"The Ten Commandments, outlined in Exodus 20, have often been interpreted as stating, 'Thou shalt not kill.' However, a more correct reading would be, 'Thou shalt not murder.' In fact, the commandment refers to a particular type of homicide that need not concern us here. When God saved the Israelites from the Pharaoh, they sang praises onto the Lord, stating, 'The Lord is a man of war; the Lord is His name.' In multiple places, Jehovah was noted to be the Lord of Hosts. This clearly means that he was the God of Battle.

"But you may ask, what about the New Testament, the New Covenant that God made with his people? My friends I would draw your attention to Luke 22:36. In that verse, Jesus tells Peter that anyone without a sword should sell his mantle and buy one. In Matthew 10:34-39, the Lord said, 'I have not come to bring peace, but a sword. For I have come to set a man against his father, and a daughter against her mother, and a daughter-in-law against her mother-in-law; and the man's foe will be those of his own household.' Thus, it will be during this war brother will fight brother and father will fight son. Beginning at Luke 12:49, Jesus stated that he came to cast fire upon the earth. People should not think that he came to give peace on Earth. No, he states that he came to cause division. Thus, there is no indication in the New Testament that the Lord Jesus had any objection to a just war.

"I will now touch upon a subject that has caused much division. The Old Testament mentions the term 'servants,' which is sometimes interpreted as 'slaves.' However, the texts are equally clear that these so-called slaves were akin to indentured servants. Although their indenture was to last for seven times seven years, at most, they were to be freed upon the year of the jubilee.

"Even assuming that God condoned slavery, that is not the case in the New Testament. The New Covenant speaks otherwise. I need not remind you that the Lord Jesus did not own slaves. Neither did members of his family, his friends, or his disciples.

"In 1 Corinthians, chapter 12, verse 13, the Lord spoke, saying, 'For by one spirit we were all baptized into one body—Jews or Greeks, slaves or free—and all were made to drink of one spirit.' At Galatians, chapter 4, verses 27 and 28, it is noted that 'for as many of you as were baptized into Christ have been put on Christ. There is neither Jew nor Greek, there's neither slave nor free . . . 'In Colossians, chapter 4, verse 11, Jesus spoke, saying, 'Here, there cannot be Greek and Jew, circumcised and uncircumcised, barbarian, Scythian, slave, free men, but Christ is all and in all.'

"Thus, my friends, it is clear that our Lord Jesus did not distinguish between slave and free men. As Christians, we must follow his footsteps. We must eradicate the curse of slavery so that all men may be free.

"Note, my friends, that I stated that the Negro should be free. I did not indicate that he is equal. I know many of you are worried that the black man will take your jobs. Clearly, this should be no concern unless you are a field hand. The fact that the slaves should be free does not indicate that they should be equal, be allowed to vote, or that they should be able to intermarry.

"So, my friends, it is clear that neither the Old or New testaments prohibit Christians from engaging in a just war. It is equally clear that, as Christians, we must make war to save the Union and free the slave. Once free, the former slaves need not be equal under the law, and fears of them having the upper hand in any endeavor are unjustified."

The last speaker of the day was Henry Winder, none other than the father of Jacob's girlfriend. He was recognized as the leader of the local Republican Party and a fair to middling orator. He began, "My friends, fellow Americans, and patriots, I want you to imagine in your mind's eye a high hill. And upon that high hill lies a gleaming tabernacle. When the rays of God's sun hit that tabernacle, they are reflected throughout the world. The result is that thousands of people from every corner of the earth are attracted to that tabernacle. I tell you, my friends, that tabernacle is our Union, the United States."

His voice began to rise as he pumped his fists in the air. "I tell you, my friends, within that tabernacle lies an altar. It is the altar of freedom! During times of war that altar demands a sacrifice of blood." His fists came down hard upon the railing. "My friends, during the War of Independence, our troops were outmanned by the greatest empire in the world. They were outnumbered and outgunned. They had virtually no navy compared to that of the British Empire. Yet the spirit of our patriots won the day. During the War of 1812, our patriots were again outmanned and outgunned. But again, the spirit of freedom moved them to defeat the mightiest empire in the world. Today, the enemies of our dear Union and freedom are the villains of the South. These people once fought side by side with our ancestors to maintain our country. Now they have turned their guns upon their brothers, upon our sacred Union. And again, the British Empire lurks in the background as a possible foe.

"However, I tell you, my friends, that today it is the patriots who have superior numbers and superior armaments. We have the industrial might and we have the navy. If the patriots' pride was sufficient to win when we were outmanned, we surely will win when we have the advantage. As pointed out by Reverend Hess, we are on God's side in this endeavor. Southerners are poor fighters. One need look no further that our War of Independence to see that the British abandoned fighting in the North and turned to the South, where they experienced great success. With God's might, our industrial power, and the bravery of our patriotic boys, I can assure you of a swift and total victory."

The crowd was in a frenzy.

Winder continued on. "My friends, to conclude our program today our band has prepared a medley of three patriotic songs. Our local newspaper has been kind enough to print the lyrics of these songs so that we all may sing along. The first song commemorates a great American patriot and fellow abolitionist. I tell you, my friends, he was the first martyr in the oncoming war. Please join me now in singing 'John Brown's Body.'"

> John Brown's body lies a-mold'ring in the grave
> John Brown's body lies a-mold'ring in the grave
> John Brown's body lies a-mold'ring in the grave
> His soul goes marching on
> Glory, Glory! Hallelujah!
> Glory, Glory! Hallelujah!
> Glory, Glory! Hallelujah!
> His soul is marching on
> He captured Harper's Ferry with his nineteen
>   men so true
> He frightened old Virginia till she trembled
>   through and through
> They hung him for a traitor, themselves the
>   traitor crew
> His soul is marching on
> Glory, Glory! Hallelujah!
> Glory, Glory! Hallelujah!
> Glory, Glory! Hallelujah!
> His soul is marching on
> John Brown died that the slave might be free,
> John Brown died that the slave might be free,
> John Brown died that the slave might be free,

But his soul is marching on!
Glory, Glory! Hallelujah!
Glory, Glory! Hallelujah!
Glory, Glory! Hallelujah!
His soul is marching on
The stars above in heaven are looking kindly
    down
The stars above in heaven are looking kindly
    down
The stars above in heaven are looking kindly
    down
On the grave of old John Brown
Glory, Glory! Hallelujah!
Glory, Glory! Hallelujah!
Glory, Glory! Hallelujah!
His soul is marching on.

It was plain to all those surrounding Winder that he could not carry a tune in a bucket. However, he persisted. "Now, my friends, please join with me in singing a new tune entitled 'May God Save the Union.'"

May God save the Union? God grant it to stand
    the pride of our people, the boast of our land
still 'mid the storm may our banner float free
unrent and unriven o'er earth and o'er sea.

May God save the Union! We trust in its might,
    in time of the tempest, in fear and in flight,
we'll fail not, we'll faint not if still in the sky
    we see all the stars in the azure field fly.

May God save the Union! Still, still may it stand
upheld by the strength of the patriot hand
to cement it our fathers ensanguined the sod,
to keep it we kneel to a merciful god.

May God save the Union! The Red,
White, and Blue,
our states keep united the dreary day through,
let the stars tell the tale of the glorious past
and bind us in Union forever to last.

"My fellow patriots, our concluding number comes from our neighboring state of Maryland. It was created during the War of 1812, when the last enemy troops set foot upon our holy ground. The lyrics to this song were written in 1814. Please join me in singing the first and last verses of 'The Star-Spangled Banner.'"

Oh, say can you see by the dawn's early light
What so proudly we hailed
at the twilight's last gleaming?
Whose broad stripes and bright stars through
the perilous fight,
O'er the ramparts we watched
were so gallantly streaming?
And the rockets' red glare, the bombs
bursting in air,
Gave proof through the night that our flag
was still there.
Oh, say does that star-spangled banner yet wave
O'er the land of the free and the home
of the brave?

Oh! Thus be it ever, when freemen shall stand
Between their loved home
and the war's desolation!
Blest with victory and peace,
may the heav'n rescued land
Praise the Power that hath made
and preserved us a nation.
Then conquer we must,
when our cause it is just,
And this be our motto: "In God is our trust."
And the star-spangled banner
in triumph shall wave
O'er the land of the free and the home
of the brave!

By the time the song had ended, there was nary a dry eye in the audience. As the people began to return home, Winder concluded, "My friends, I ask you: could an unjust cause be the inspiration for such glorious music? Nay, I say, nay, a thousand times nay."

As we know today, the war was not short, and the victory was not swift. The war dragged on, and the administration took steps that would both significantly undercut and support the war effort.

Chapter III

THE POINT OF NO RETURN

The early victory promised by Mr. Winder never materialized. The war skipped through 1861, 1862, and 1863. To make things worse, the North was struggling. The Union's advantage in terms of men and materiel was trumped by the South's esprit de corps and the ingenuity of rebel officers.

Still, the Confederacy was not without its problems. Its chronic lack of manpower came to a head in 1862. As a result, the Confederate legislature in Richmond adopted conscription. This met with resistance in North Carolina, South Carolina, Tennessee, and West Virginia. Moreover, draftees were regarded as unpatriotic because they had not volunteered for military service.

On January 1, 1863, Lincoln administration issued the Emancipation Proclamation. This took the Democrats and the conservative wing of the Republican Party by surprise. Ostensibly, the proclamation freed all the slaves in the states that were in rebellion. It was strangely silent on the status of slaves in the border states that had not seceded. The proclamation set off a political firestorm.

Within the Commonwealth, the Senate held twenty-one Republicans and twelve Democrats. The House had forty-five Republicans and fifty-five Democrats. On April 13, 1863, the Pennsylvania House of Representatives passed a resolution.

"That this General Assembly in exercise of its right to differ with the Federal Executive, enters its solemn protest against the Proclamation of the President of the United States . . . by which he assumed to emancipate slaves in certain states, holding the same to be unwise, unconstitutional and void."

In early February 1863, Alexander Patton of Greene County introduced a resolution to stop supplying men and matériel until the proclamation was rescinded. Later that month, John Ellis of Columbia County sought a resolution for a Constitution convention to restore the Union. In meetings held in Columbia County in April 1863, President Lincoln was compared to the tsar. Abolition was said to be morally and socially wrong as well as unconstitutional. On April 18, 1863, the *Columbia County Democrat* published an article charging that Lincoln had now made this "a Nigger War." It was the opinion of the editor that "Negroes were better off in bondage and enslaved as it was the will of God."

From Wilkes-Barre in Luzerne County came the following poem:

> We are taxed for our clothing, our meat and our bread on our carpets and dishes our tables and beds, on our tea and our coffee our fuel and our lights, and we're taxed so severely that we can't sleep o'nights, and all this for the nigger, great God! can this be the land of the brave and the home of the free.

The *Columbia County Democrat* concluded, "Lincoln's declaration that he will end the war on the basis of freedom of the Negro . . . stands in the light of an unmitigated crime. If Lincoln is reelected, Johnny will never come marching home."

The so-called Peace Democrats or Copperheads held a four-to-one majority in the northern townships of Columbia County, including Benton, Sugarloaf, and Fishing Creek. Although there were a few blacks within the Commonwealth, the Emancipation Proclamation set off a panic, as blacks were seen as being paupers, criminals, and, at best, job competition.

Fort Sumter was fired upon on April 12, 1861. Three days later came a request for seventy-five thousand volunteers. This request and subsequent calls raised half a million volunteers. In September 1862, the Confederates invaded Maryland, and a levy en masse was called in Pennsylvania. On September 15, 1862, "emergency men" left Bloomsburg. Another contingent left on September 22. By June 1863, Columbia County had sent approximately five companies to serve in the Union army. These early "calls" were primarily for volunteers and were made on a state-by-state basis. In mid-April 1861, President Lincoln had called for fourteen regiments to be raised in Pennsylvania. The number of volunteers exceeded this amount, and the excess volunteers became reservists. By December 1862, the Commonwealth sent seventy-one thousand volunteers to serve in the Union army, filling 193 regiments.

Pennsylvania was divided into the Department of Susquehanna under General Darius N. Couch and the Department of Monongahela under General W. D. H. Brooks. On June 28, 1863, General George Meade was placed in command of all Union forces.

By late June 1863, rebel forces under General John B. Gordon of the Georgia Brigade advanced within two miles south of York. He was repulsed by General George A. Custer of the Michigan Brigade at Hanover. Advance forces under

General Lee were within sight of the capital at Harrisburg but turned south to meet General Meade. The Northern Army of the Potomac with eighty-five thousand men and General Lee with seventy-five thousand men met at Gettysburg, a small town containing several strategic roads. Initially, two Pennsylvania brigades held Seminary Ridge costing a heavy death toll for the 150th Pennsylvania Volunteers.

The rebel incursion into the Commonwealth terrorized many of its citizens. Congress concluded that the army needed to be strengthened. Congress also saw a steady decline in volunteerism since late 1862. The solution from Washington was the institution of a military draft. That draft was to include all males ages twenty to thirty-five and all unmarried males ages thirty-six to forty-five. The group of older, unmarried men was not to be called until the first group was exhausted. There were exemptions for the physically and mentally unfit, as well as those caring for aging and ailing parents and men with orphaned siblings younger than twelve and fathers of motherless children under twelve. If two members of a family were already serving, that family was entitled to two exemptions. In addition, one could pay a $300 commutation fee to avoid the draft or hire a substitute. It was argued that this consigned the poor man to the hardships and dangers of the battlefield while exempting the rich. It was called a rich man's war and a poor man's fight.

Not all citizens agreed with the government's solution to the problem. Some compared the draft to the English "press gangs" that had precipitated the War of 1812.

Stern resistance to the draft occurred in New York City. There, approximately two thousand were left dead after riots. The riots included several blacks being lynched, a case of blaming the victim.

Opponents of the draft cited Daniel Webster's 1812 statement that there was "no constitutional basis to take children from parents or parents from children."

It was also argued that the draft would destroy the state militia.

Many of the newspapers in central Pennsylvania editorialized against the draft. Franklin Wierick of *The Selinsgrove Times* was nearly lynched by a mob of local patriots. He was later placed under a $1,500 bond for treasonable statements. In late 1863, the *Northumberland County Democrat* was raided by the Forty-Sixth Pennsylvania Volunteers. Two months later, it was again raided by the Tenth New York Calvary Regiment and ransacked.

Resistance to the draft mounted. Seven members of Knights of the Golden Circle were arrested in Mifflinburg in Snyder County. They were sent to Harrisburg because a mob had formed to rescue them. Draft resisters were active in Pottsville. At Clearfield, Colonel Cyrus Butler was fatally shot, and near Lock Haven, Lieutenant Kress, a provost marshal, was seriously wounded. Near New Berlin, shots were exchanged when federal authorities attempted to arrest James Hummell. In Columbia County, a draft enforcer named Stiles was threatened with an ax and hit with a rotten egg. He awoke one morning to find a coffin on his front lawn with a sign "Hurrah for Jeff Davis". In mid-July 1863, the draft office in Troy was broken into and records stolen. Some state legislators proposed that not one more dollar or one man be given to the cause until the administration in Washington changed.

Hatred of the commutation fee grew amid charges of bribery. Lieutenant-Colonel Charles Stewart ordered Alexander Hess to pay $100 to escape arrest and be discharged from the draft. It had been established that Hess was unfit for service, having suffered a rupture. The money was paid and on

September 15, 1864, Stewart wrote the following letter: "This is to certify that I have this day examined Alexander Hess of Sugarloaf Township, Columbia County, and find him badly ruptured and unfit for service in the Armies of the United States." Lieutenant-Colonel Stewart then signed the letter. This seems to be an obvious case of bribery as it was beyond Colonel Stewart's authority to make such examinations and grant such deferments.

Colonel John Freeze complained about the high draft quota for Columbia County. He also noted that an undue number of Democrats appeared on the draft list. He argued that the county should be credited for local recruits enlisting in other counties that offered higher bounties. The response from the local provost marshal, Captain Manville, was that an undue number of Democrats appeared on the draft list because so few had volunteered for service. An inordinate number of Republicans volunteered and were not subject to the draft; accordingly, a disproportionate number of Democrats were subject to the draft.

John Freeze was not only a military man but also an attorney. He appealed his case to Washington. He did not receive a response until March 15, 1865.

Dear Sir:

The Provost Marshal General of the United States, after sending up an agent to investigate the enrollment in your district and receiving his report, has removed Captain Manville, the Provost Marshal, and has ordered the draft to proceed upon the basis of an enrollment of six thousand, which is a reduction of nearly one-half

> from the enrollment before any adjustment and
> must materially reduce our quota.
>
> I am truly yours,
> H. W. Tract

The draft act was known as an act for enrolling and calling out national forces. Three conscripts from the Commonwealth sued the federal government and the provost marshal to prevent their forced entry into the military. The case was argued before the State Supreme Court on September 23, 1863, in Philadelphia. The court was made up of four Democrats and one Republican. George A. Coffee, U.S. district attorney, failed to appear. The federal government assumed that the State Supreme Court had no authority to rule on an issue of federal law. In an unusual move, former President James Buchanan wrote to Justice George Woodward, a Democrat on the court, asking that the court uphold the draft law. Woodward would be the Democrat candidate for governor in a later election. On November 9, 1863, Chief Justice Walter N. Lowrie read the opinion of the court. By a three-to-two vote, the court decided that Congress could raise and support armies as noted in the Constitution. However, absent specific authority to draft, the federal government had to rely upon the state militias to raise an army. Thus, the state court attempted to strike down the federal draft law. Justice Woodward issued a separate opinion stating that Congress had no power to draft members of the state militia. Justice James Thompson, another Democrat, wrote that the draft act would destroy state militias. Only Justices William Strong, a Democrat, and John Read, the Republican, voted to uphold the draft. On January 16, 1864, Judge Lowrie was replaced by Judge Daniel Agnew. The court took another vote and vacated the temporary injunction prohibiting conscription of the plaintiffs.

It was estimated that by 1864, three quarters of the drafted men in the northern-tier townships of Columbia County failed to appear for induction. It was rumored that during the daytime, draft resisters identified each other by running their hand along their collar. They were also to identify themselves by knocking on a door three times. The person inside would respond with the word "bear" and the person outside would likewise respond with the same word. They would both then say, "wolf."

The federal authorities could not allow the deserters and draft dodgers to go unchallenged. To do so would encourage others to follow in their footsteps. If this happened, the constant stream of men necessary to prosecute the war effort would evaporate. Something had to be done, and it had to be done now.

In July 1864, Deputy Provost Marshal Solomon Taylor of Fairmont Township in Luzerne County enlisted six men, including Lieutenant James Stewart Robinson, who had recently returned from three years of war to seek out deserters and draft evaders in northern Columbia County. To the locals, this group would be known as Lincoln's Midnight Raiders.

At daybreak, the troops saddled up and crossed into Columbia County. There were jokes and snide comments made about the Copperheads they were about to apprehend. They also cajoled Lieutenant Robinson to tell the story of how he was captured by the rebels and later escaped. At times, they moved quietly, with only the sounds of horses' hooves and the clanking of handcuffs and leg irons. At one point, the troops shared a chuckle as a grouse ran beside them with her wing dragging on the ground. They had all seen it before and knew what was coming. When the grouse had reached a point safely from her nest, she tucked in the wing, flapped both wings, and took off. It was simply a feint, in an attempt to draw the men away from her nest.

The first man on their list was Thomas Smith, an alleged deserter. Fortunately for Smith, his wife spotted the posse long before they reached the farmhouse. She alerted her husband who jumped out the back window and escaped into a cornfield. Next, she loosed the dogs on the soldiers and then proceeded to the second floor, threw open a window, and blew a horn to warn the neighbors. The sound of horns and clanging tubs could be heard throughout the valley. The meaning of the clamor was unmistakable: there was a federal posse in the area.

At first, the posse considered shooting the dogs and then decided to proceed so long as the dogs did not actually bite them or their horses. Mrs. Smith denied seeing her husband as of late and simply drew a blank as to when she had seen him last or where he was going. Perhaps he had gone into town to buy supplies or had gone to visit neighbors.

The story was much the same at each farmhouse. Friends, relatives, and neighbors could not recollect seeing any of the wanted men. Amazingly, a goodly number were reported to be out of state visiting relatives. The day proved fruitless, with not one arrest made.

By sundown, the troops were exhausted, hot, and frustrated. They had just reached a bend in the road near what was then the Ravens Creek Post Office when they saw a group of men coming toward them. Lieutenant Robinson moved to the lead and yelled, "Halt or we'll shoot." The response came back, "Well, shoot it is." Exactly who fired the first shot is unknown. However, Lieutenant Robinson felt a sharp pain in his left arm, followed by another in his right shoulder. It felt as though he was being struck with hot irons. His horse turned sideways in the road, and he felt a sharp pain in his stomach. At that point, things went blank, and he fell from his horse. Two members of the posse stayed to assist him while the remaining members gave chase, but to no avail. The shooters knew the terrain and quickly evaporated into the deer trails and valleys.

Members of the posse returned to find Lieutenant Robinson mortally wounded. He was hit seven times. Lieutenant Robinson made a valiant effort at recovery but died thirteen and a half weeks later due to peritonitis. He was twenty-nine years old.

Lieutenant Robinson was buried at the Bethel Hill Cemetery with the following inscription on his grave: "Was shot by a Rebel sympathizer in Benton Township, Columbia County, Pennsylvania, while assisting a U.S. officer in attempting to arrest deserters July 31st and died of wounds, November 30, 1864." The Robinson grave site in Fairmont, Luzerne County, is a few miles from Ricketts Glen State Park. He had been a veteran of Fredericksburg and held prisoner after the Battle of the Wilderness in May 1864 but had escaped. Other members of the posse were Eli Buckalew, Isaac Harrison, Robert Montgomery, Charles Dodson, and two men named Russell and Long.

Several of the shooters fled to Canada and did not return until after the war. Local authorities took no action, and the incident was considered to be a dead case. However, twenty-seven years later, a boundary dispute arose. At that point, one of the litigants named Elias Young as Lieutenant Robinson's killer. Captain John Robinson, the brother of Lieutenant Robinson, made the arrest. The trial was held in September 1891 in Luzerne County Courthouse.

To say the least, the testimony was conflicting and confusing. The twenty-seven-year delay in the trial did not help. Basically, it was determined that the defendant, Elias Young, was courting Peggy Smith when he heard that the soldiers were in the area and were going to arrest her brother, Thomas Smith, as a "drafted man." Reportedly, Elias obtained a gun from Richard Smith.

Charles Dodson, one of the posse, testified that Taylor, another member of the posse, yelled, "No firing." He asserted that the oncoming party fired only three shots and were later chased for one-quarter mile. How Lieutenant Robinson could have been hit seven times if only three shots were fired was not explained.

Thomas Smith testified that Young had taken his gun and admitted that he had used it. He stated that he was in the party that included Young and his own brother, Minor Smith. However, Young testified that he and his companions were returning from swimming. When they saw the posse approaching them, they assumed that they were going to be robbed. Thomas Smith not only testified that Young had fired a gun, but he also stated that he (Young) had seen a man fall. Richard Hess, another member of the party, testified that Young told him that he was the only one who had fired any shots. Young's basic defense was that of self-defense. The testimony was conflicting on what type of weapon Young had and what type of bullet or shot had killed Lieutenant Robinson. Some testimony indicated that Lieutenant Robinson had been hit with rifle fire while others said it was a pistol shot or buckshot. The jury deliberated from 5:45-9:30 p.m. and returned a verdict of not guilty.

After the shooting, rumors began that a group of Copperheads, probably Knights of the Golden Circle, drafted men, deserters, and Confederate regulars were amassing at

North Mountain. Further rumors indicated that they had acquired two pieces of heavy artillery and were going to open a second front behind Union lines. Apparently, no one stopped to consider how rebel forces would lug two canons through Virginia, Maryland, and most of Pennsylvania without being detected. In any case, the provost marshal reported the rumors as fact. In addition, a cavalry officer maintained that there were from three hundred to five hundred drafted men in the northern townships who would most likely be willing to join them. The rumors were presented as fact and made their way up the chain of command. The authorities in Harrisburg and Washington conferred. The decision was made: troops would be sent in to put down the rebels.

Chapter IV

INVASION

The first troops arrived in Bloomsburg in early August 1864. They consisted of eight cavalry, forty infantry, and were accompanied by two cannons. They were shortly joined by Captain Bruce Lambert's independent company of mounted men, one section of the Keystone Battery from Philadelphia under the command of Lieutenant Roberts, and a battalion of infantry commanded by Lieutenant-Colonel Stewart. Shortly thereafter followed a battalion of the Veteran Reserves Corps and 250 more soldiers under the command of Major-General Darius N. Couch.

The troops camped south of Bloomsburg, in the area that is now the fairgrounds. This gave them access to the road running northward through Bloomsburg, Lightstreet, Orangeville, and Benton. Just to the west of the road ran a good stream that provided adequate water for the troops. The enlisted men were limited to the campground except for occasional trips into town to obtain goods. The officers were given free rein to go into town whenever they were not on duty. When they did so, they found a typical mid-nineteenth-century small town with a flourishing economy with everything from millinery shops to blacksmith shops. If there was anything odd, it was the absence of men of age for military service.

Military intelligence reported that there were two to three hundred rebel troops along with draft dodgers on North

Mountain in the southern part of Luzerne County. They also reported that they had two or three cannons with them. Radical Republicans insisted there were hundreds, or possibly thousands, of rebels armed and organized, accompanied by refugees and deserters from Canada up in the hills. The Reverend Reuben E. Wilson gave a speech in Milton. He stated there were thousands of rebel troops up Fishing Creek and that they were armed and dangerous. He said they attempted to set fire to Bloomsburg several times and did manage to burn down a stable. The truth was that no one had tried to torch Bloomsburg. True, a stable had been set afire, but by boys playing with matches. Others spread rumors that draft dodgers were hiding in dugout porches and other fake outbuildings, such as outhouses and pigsties.

Also, there was a large group of Copperheads, or Southern sympathizers, in the townships in the northern tier of Columbia County. Originally, they were called Copperheads because they were known to place a copper penny in their front window to express their opposition to the war. Another group was known as the Knights of the Golden Circle. They also resisted the war, but their last recorded meeting was in May 1863. At that time, they raised $700 for draft bounties. This would allow men to purchase an exemption to the draft. Except for the shooting of Lieutenant Stewart Robinson, this was the extent of the violent resistance.

The Union officers realized the potential for a violent confrontation. Therefore, they felt it would be best to have some local officials on their side. When it came to local officials, one name stood out: United States Senator Charles R. Buckalew. The senator was one of nine children born to John McKinley Buckalew and his wife, Martha Funston. He was educated at the Franklin Academy and excelled in writing and oratory. Failing to find work as an engineer, he studied law under Mordicae Jackson of Berwick. In 1845, Buckalew found work as a deputy attorney general. He spoke at numerous temperance meetings and believed in American expansion and white supremacy.

Senator Buckalew was a well-liked moderate Democratic politician from Columbia County. He had held local offices and was elected to the state legislature. In those days, state legislators elected United States senators. In 1862, the Pennsylvania Senate had twenty-one Republicans and twelve Democrats, while the House had fifty-five Democrats and forty-five Republicans. The Republicans were split into two wings, one headed by Governor Andrew Gregg Curtin and the other by Senator Simon Cameron, a turncoat Democrat. Several years before, three Democrats had defected to elect Cameron to the United States Senate. This outraged Democratic leaders, especially those in Philadelphia. It was declared that, should any future Democratic legislator defect, they would not be allowed to leave the halls of the statehouse in Harrisburg alive. As luck would have it, Buckalew became the next Democratic candidate for the Senate. To enforce their threat, Democratic leaders from Philadelphia sent armed assassins to the capital in Harrisburg. These men actually walked the halls of the state capitol and grounds to intimidate any Democratic legislator from defecting to the Republican side. John Cessna, the Democratic Speaker of the House, and George V. Lawrence, the Republican head of the Senate, asked federal authorities for protection. Alexander McClure, the assistant adjutant general of the United States and military commander of the Harrisburg area, refused. He took great delight explaining to Representative John Cessna that the issue of murder, or potential murder, was one of state rights. Certainly, a Democrat could understand the importance of state rights and the need to keep federal authorities out of the state business, especially the legislature. After all, if there was a shooting, the Commonwealth would have one less politician and one less Democratic politician at that.

Representative Schofield, a Democrat from Philadelphia, alleged that during the vote he had been offered $100,000 to vote for a Republican but refused. As a result of all this, voting was strictly on party lines, and Buckalew was elected to the United States Senate by a vote of sixty-seven to sixty-six. At the time, Buckalew had been a member of the legislature since 1852. He was a quiet man, and it was felt he had little or no knowledge of political strategy. He was a cold and an unimpassioned speaker. He was reputed to be a strict constructionist of the Constitution, and his major qualities were purity of character and his ability to speak in a logical and forceful manner. Once in the Senate he was respected by his Republican colleagues. He was so well respected that in 1872, he was nominated for the governorship of Pennsylvania by liberal Republicans. Although he never became governor, he later served two terms in Congress.

To begin their public relations campaign, Major General Couch mounted his horse and, unescorted, rode to Cedar Hill just outside of Bloomsburg, the home of Senator Buckalew. The general reached the farmhouse but was told that Senator Buckalew was out in the fields. Couch dismounted and tied his horse to a hitching post. He then walked out into the fields, where he found a group of men harvesting hay. Some were working by hand, and some were using a strange-looking machine. As the general walked downhill toward the men, his sword dug small furrows into the ground. He had gone no more than a few hundred feet when he began perspiring. Beneath his breath, he began to curse. Those damned Confederate officers had unlimited access to cotton. Oh, what he would have given to be able to design his own tunic and trousers from that cool material.

Upon reaching the men, he called out that he was looking for Senator Buckalew. One of the men working in the field turned and walked toward the general. He was a rather short, frail man with a receding hairline, thick neck, and deep-set eyes. The man was clean-shaven and naked from the waist up. As he approached the general, he reached for the straps of his suspenders that had been dangling below his waist and pulled them over his shoulders. "Well, you found him," said the man. The general was dumbfounded. He had always assumed that a person such as a United States senator would be rather tall and most likely have a beard.

Senator Buckalew saw his surprise. "Well, I see you're somewhat shocked to see a senator working in the fields. I've just purchased this newfangled reaping equipment and decided we'd have a little contest between the horse and machine on one hand and the field hands on the other. I must say the machine appears to be winning. I am loath to let any of my men go, so I suppose I will have to find other jobs for them. What can I do for you?" asked the senator.

"As you know," said Couch, "we have several troops bivouacked just south of Bloomsburg and are about to move north against a contingent of draft dodgers and rebels in the North Mountain area. We feel it would be best to get the support of some local leaders before doing so, so as to minimize the chances of unnecessary violence."

"I can assure you, general, there is no armed resistance in any part of this county," the senator replied. "However, if you would like, I would be willing to ride with you and your troops in order to minimize the chances of any violent confrontation."

The general was not too keen on the possibility of having a United States senator shot while in his protection. He responded, "It is not necessary for you to accompany the troops, sir. However, it would be nice if you could say a few kind words about us to the local political leaders. In addition, it would also be of help if you could suggest a local political leader, one of lesser note, who might accompany us."

The senator scratched his head and thought for a moment and then said, "Well, there is a Colonel John Freeze who is a friend of mine and well-liked by most people in the county. In addition, he has some military experience and is somewhat familiar with the terrain in the northern part of the county. Perhaps he would accompany you."

The general was somewhat taken aback. Other than Colonel Hiram Kline, who was supposedly the head of the rebel forces, Colonel Freeze had been named as one of the major rebel sympathizers in the area. "Senator, it is our information that Colonel Kline is the ring leader of the rebels holed up in North Mountain and that Colonel Freeze is sympathetic to that cause," Couch said.

The senator replied that the allegations regarding Colonel Kline were inconsistent with the man's character, as he knew it.

"And what of Colonel Freeze? Well, perhaps it would be best if Colonel Freeze and I would meet with you tomorrow at your headquarters," Buckalew suggested.

"That sounds like a splendid suggestion," stated the general. "In that case, I bid you adieu and look forward to seeing you again."

Before the meeting the next day, Republican leaders spoke with General Couch and warned him that Senator Buckalew was a moderate Democrat, but still a Democrat. In addition, it was stated that Colonel Freeze had often expressed antiwar sentiments. When Colonel Freeze arrived, General Couch asked if he would take a message to the nonreporting drafted men in the northern part of the county. At first, Colonel Freeze declined but then reconsidered. The general's message to the draft resisters was that penalties for draft resistance and desertion would be remitted, but only if the culprits immediately reported to the provost marshal. This idea was approved by Senator Buckalew and eventually accepted by Colonel Freeze.

Colonel Freeze then made a counteroffer: he would take General Couch by carriage so they might both hunt for the alleged fortification and cannons. Colonel Freeze pledged the safety of the party, but General Couch declined. Shortly thereafter, General Couch returned to Harrisburg, leaving Lieutenant-Colonel Stewart in command. Stewart also declined Colonel Freeze's offer to tour the northern-tier townships. After all, a cavalry officer had reported, "Certain knowledge, there were five hundred nonreporting men up the creek." Word of the meeting spread quickly, but there were no takers for the offer of amnesty.

On Sunday, August 21, 1864, several hundred troops under the command of Lieutenant-Colonel Stewart marched through Bloomsburg and headed north. Colonel Stewart headed up the force, with cavalry and the American flag right behind him. Immediately behind them followed a fife and drum corps. It was a beautiful day with flags snapping in the breeze and the sun glinting off musical instruments and bayonets.

The scene was reminiscent of the First Battle of Bull Run. Many locals, already dressed in their best Sunday go-to-meeting clothes, followed the troops. Several boys ran alongside the troops, pointing out various insignia of rank and unit. Most were just inaccurate guesses, but it provided good entertainment for the boys. Several men followed on horseback, and there were carriages with whole families. Some of the revelers followed the troops past Lightstreet and on toward Orangeville. At the end of the first day, the troops bivouacked at the intersection of the main road and Stucker's Bottom. The next day, they camped at Applemen's Bottom near Benton. By Tuesday, the contingent was approximately five hundred strong. Several friendly locals donated baskets of food to the troops. Late Tuesday night and early Wednesday morning, the troops surrounded several houses, including that of Jacob Saddler. As noted earlier, this resulted in the arrest of nearly one hundred civilians, with forty-five of them being detained and sent by train to Philadelphia.

On Sunday, General George Cadwalader arrived in Bloomsburg. He immediately moved northward to reinforce Lieutenant-Colonel Stewart. General Cadwalader had approximately five hundred troops with him, bringing the total contingent of Union troops to roughly a thousand. His men fanned out to Stillwater, Sugarloaf, and Jackson Townships, as well as Cambria and New Columbus Townships in Luzerne County.

After the men were shipped off to Philadelphia, the troops regrouped at the foot of North Mountain. The soldiers headed out into left, center, and right columns and began their assault on North Mountain. The valiant troops charged up the mountain against fortifications of berry brambles, hazarding scratches, and stubbed toes. In fact, there were some casualties. While climbing up the mountain, one Union trooper placed his hand on a ledge for support. He heard some movement, but the sound did not register in his mind fast enough for him to withdraw his hand. He was bitten by a large copperhead snake and carried down the mountain by his companions. Eventually, he lost two fingers. He was to be the only casualty caused by "copperheads." In addition, another soldier lost his balance and fell, breaking an ankle. There were also various scrapes and bruises from climbing through briars and some cases of dehydration and sunstroke. After several hours of climbing and searching, they found no more than a few youngsters at a picnic in the middle of what General Cadwalader described as a huckleberry patch. For over a week his men continued to hunt for the alleged artillery and fortifications. However, nothing was found. At best, they found an old slate heap with a few chutes that had been abandoned, to be picked up later, should the market for slate improve. It would take a person with extremely bad eyesight, or in a drunken stupor, to mistake this for fortifications with cannons. After the "battle," the troops retired to Coleman's farm above Stillwater.

Cadwalader was furious and stormed back to Bloomsburg. He told Senator Buckalew that the whole campaign was a complete farce. Senator Buckalew could not help but smile, as he had originally informed the authorities that there was no organized armed resistance within the county.

Later, one Captain William Silvers filled out an affidavit proclaiming, "I further swear that in all my searches through Columbia and Sullivan Counties, I never found a trace of earthworks or fortifications, nor did I have any knowledge of artillery to resist the draft under state troops." The troops were to linger for months in the northern part of the county. There were complaints of wooden fences being used for firewood, corn being used to feed the troops and horses, and other minor problems. There were no major problems, such as shootings, rape, or barn burning. However, there was one incident that was to anger the community for years to come.

During the search for rebels, draft dodgers, and deserters, the troopers fell upon the farm of Leonard Cole. He was nowhere to be found, but they latched upon his young son, also named Leonard. While his mother was held in the modest farmhouse, a sergeant and several soldiers dragged Leonard into the barn. A rope was thrown over a rafter and Leonard was threatened with hanging if he did not reveal the location of his father. Tears welled in his eyes, and he could not speak; the boy simply shook his head no. The sergeant in charge, the same sergeant that had arrested Jacob Saddler, had the noose placed around the boy's neck. He was asked one last time for his father's whereabouts but again refused to comply. Two soldiers were then ordered to pull the rope, and the boy was slowly lifted off the ground. His feet swung wildly in the air, looking for traction that was not to be found. The boy's lips turned blue and his face became ashen. His tongue began to swell and his eyes bulged. At that point, a loud ruckus was heard coming up the road. The officer in charge entered the barn. He immediately noted the potential for twin disasters: the killing of the young boy and firing on civilians. He ordered that the boy be let down and he was. Apparently, a large group of neighbors, armed primarily with farm implements, was fast approaching. The Union troops left the boy on the floor of the barn and hightailed it to safer areas. Young Leonard lived through the experience but lost his vision. He died a few months later, and his death was blamed on residual effects from the hanging. This resulted in bitter resentment of Union troops throughout the area, even by some who originally supported their presence.

Some of the troops left to track down deserters and draft dodgers, conducting raids in Berks, Clearfield, Pike, and Schuylkill Counties. The last troops did not leave until December 1, 1864. What the Army of the Fishing Creek did during the remainder of their occupation of Columbia County will be told later.

In 1924, the Wilkes-Barre Sunday *Independent* reported that Charles Rice of Luzerne County had summed up the Battle of North Mountain as follows:

> The trained army, fully equipped with the panoply of war that was to march up the gurgling mocking Fishingcreek through shocked and afrightened villages, past scattered homesteads to capture the rifle pits that were never dug, to arrest deserters who never deserted, to hurl its proud strength against a mirage as illusionary as any that ever lured across desert sands against a phantom fort manned by phantom rebels.

Rice had been the judge at the trial of Elias Young.

Chapter V

THE RANTZ MEETING

Most Bloomsburg residents welcomed the presence of Union troops camped just south of town. They formed a bulwark against whatever demons might be lurking in the northern part of the county. In addition, any needs not provided for by the army were taken care of by local merchants. The presence of federal troops was to provide a temporary boon to the local economy.

Most people living in the northern part of the county did not share this view. The presence of federal troops with the avowed purpose of rounding up drafted men and deserters was bad enough. Many residents feared the troops would go further and round up local dissidents. Some also feared that the troopers would be undisciplined and burn down barns and destroy crops.

The citizens of the northern part of the county had little idea of what to do other than simply complain. However, John Rantz, a local farmer, decided to take action. By way of handwritten flyers and word of mouth, he called a meeting at his farmhouse. He felt it was time to clear the air and possibly plan to resist any incursion by Union troops.

For those traveling south toward his farm, the road would wind around a mountain toward the west. Peering down in the valley, one could see the Rantz residence that consisted of the original log cabin with a clapboard kitchen attached to the south side between the log cabin and a small stream. Downstream, to the west, a bedroom had been added. On the north side, a porch had been added to the front of the house. Underneath the porch roof was wainscoting. Further west, separate from the house, was the outhouse. Although he knew this was too close to the stream, Rantz figured this was a problem for his downstream neighbors. Further downstream was a detached barn, and just past the barn were Rantz's fields.

On the day of the meeting, men and boys arrived from the northern-tier townships as well as some from Luzerne County. Nearly every tree had a horse or wagon hitched to it. Dozens crowded into the cabin, filling the kitchen and the bedroom. Outside on the porch, people craned to hear what was going on inside. From nearly every window dangled the backsides and legs of boys. Mrs. Rantz was kept busy bringing water and feeding muffins to the participants. Ironically, Rantz would miss most of the meeting, as he was out recruiting people to attend the meeting.

The first speakers were the firebrands. They wanted to arm every available man and attack the Union troops should they move northward. Just before noon, Elton Fisher, a local attorney, took the stage. The stage was a large washtub that had been turned upside down in the middle of the old log cabin.

"My fellow citizens and neighbors, I come today to address you on a few topics, the first of which is the issue of slavery," Fisher began. "I note that the Constitution provides for slavery. In article 1, section 2, there is a provision that three-fifths of all other persons, those being slaves, will be counted for purposes of representation in Congress. Article 4, section 2 provides that any escaped slave shall not be freed or discharged from service but will be delivered up upon the claim of the slave owner. Moreover, article 1, section 9 provides that the importation of slaves was not to be prohibited by Congress prior to 1808. Please note that this leaves open the possibility that the *importation* of slaves might be prohibited after 1808. Although the importation of new slaves may or may not be prohibited, it does not say existing slaves should be free.

"In 1857, the Supreme Court of the United States issued its decision in the *Dred Scott* case. Basically, the highest court of the land ruled that slaves are nothing but chattel or personal property of the owner. A slave does not have standing as does a real person. Hence, the highest law of the land and the highest court of the land have authorized continuation of the institution of slavery. Indeed, Congress legitimized slavery when it passed the Fugitive Slave Act.

"My friends, I note that although the Lincoln administration is willing to tear the country apart and go to war over the issue of slavery, the north continues to deal with Brazil, Spain, and Turkey. All of these countries continue to practice slavery without the slightest objection from the Northern merchants.

"Slaves were first imported to the Western Hemisphere when in 1503 they were brought to Hispaniola. In 1562, an Englishman, Sir John Hawkins, took slaves to the same island. His partner in this adventure was Queen Elizabeth herself. English kings granted charters for the slave trade, and James II was a partner in such trade. In 1620, Dutch merchants brought the first slaves to the colony of Virginia."

Counselor Fisher then launched into what would today be called the ultimate supply-side economic argument. He insisted that the residents of Virginia did not want to take these slaves. However, they saw that the health of the slaves had badly deteriorated and that most of them would not survive further sea journey. Therefore, they reluctantly purchased such slaves, he said. Once they had them in custody, they decided to recoup their money by putting them to work. No one in the audience asked why Dutch merchants would go to the trouble and spend money to hire or rent a ship and supply a crew. The ship and crew then had to make the voyage to Africa, where they had to spend more money to purchase slaves or engage in the risky endeavor of capturing them. Following that would be a dangerous voyage across the Atlantic all to sell slaves in a market that apparently did not exist.

He continued, "In the Treaty of Utrecht in 1712, Queen Anne of Spain ceded the slave trade between Africa and the Americas. The English crown abandoned its monopoly on the slave trade in 1749, allowing all English merchants to ship slaves. The Puritans engaged in killing and enslaving Indians. Indeed, the first American slave ship was *The Desire*, captained by a merchant from Salem, Massachusetts."

Attorney Fisher argued that on numerous occasions the people of Virginia tried to outlaw the importation of slaves but were overturned by the king and parliament. In the original draft of the Declaration of Independence, Thomas Jefferson noted that the king had supported the slave trade against the will of the colonies. However, this portion was deleted at the insistence of Georgia and South Carolina. The Confederate Constitution banned the importation of slaves as it was felt that too many slaves would flood the market and lower their value.

Fisher noted that the slave trade would have been virtually impossible had it not been for the slave merchants and slave ships sailing from New England.

"At one point," Fisher said, "most European nations were slaveholding nations, and English judges declared slaves to be mere merchandise. In 1778, George Washington objected to Britain taking fugitive slaves back to England. In 1788, the United States government demanded that Spain return fugitive slaves who had fled to Florida. In 1815, the Treaty of Ghent provided for indemnity for slaves taken in the War of Independence and the War of 1812. At one point, all of the colonies were slaveholding under English law as were the territories acquired from France. In 1772, the *Somerset* case, a case in British common law, Lord Mansfield stated there were fifteen thousand black slaves in England. Under English law, debtors could have their slaves taken from them in payment for debt. Not only had the colonies inherited legitimate slave trade from the British, but it also had been legalized by the Constitution and court cases.

"In more recent years, the Virginia Assembly has considered the abolition of slavery. Although none of these bills passed, it shows that there was a constant agitation to end this practice. As all states had been slaveholding states at one point and as the Northern states had abolished slavery, it is apparent that, given time, the Southern states may well have followed suit. However, Lincoln and the abolitionists would not wait. Rather than negotiate, their solution was war.

"In the year 1776, there were approximately ten thousand slaves in the Commonwealth of Pennsylvania. On March 1, 1780, the state legislature forbade the importation of new slaves. By 1790, there were only 3,737 slaves left. This dwindled to the point that by 1840 there were only sixty-four slaves left.

"My friends, I will now briefly address the issue of secession. After the War of Independence, the individual states voluntarily joined the Union. There is nothing in the Constitution of United States that prohibits such states from voluntarily leaving the Union.

"The Lincoln administration howls about the evils of slavery. Their primary supporters are the abolitionists and

New England merchants. However, during the War of 1812, it was the fathers and grandfathers of these very New England merchants who wanted to secede from the Union. And why did they want to destroy the Union? Was it from some moral or religious principle? Nay, it was because their pocketbooks suffered without trade with England during the War of 1812. Now the same hypocrites howl when the Southern states wish to perform the very act that they felt appropriate only a few decades ago.

"Article 4, section 3 of our Constitution provides as follows: 'New States may be admitted by the Congress into this Union; but no new State shall be formed or erected within the Jurisdiction of any State; nor any State be formed by the Jurisdiction of two or more States, or Parts of States, without the Consent of the Legislatures of the States concerned as well as of Congress.' However, these same fine gentlemen of Congress had no qualms about violating the Constitution when the current state of West Virginia was ripped from the southern state of Virginia. The state of Virginia never consented to this abhorrent and unconstitutional act.

"The current abolitionists like to brag about how many men have volunteered to serve in the Union army. However, let's take a closer look at this. The 178th Regiment was raised primarily from Columbia County. However, I tell you there is widespread opposition to military service, and such opposition is growing. In Company A of the 178th Regiment, twenty-one men were discharged or given surgeon's certificates so that they no longer had to serve. In addition, there were five deserters. In Company H, twenty-four men deserted, and nine were released on surgeon's certificates. In Company I, twelve were released on surgeon's certificates and thirteen deserted. From the noted Thirty-Fifth Regiment, Sixth Reserves, the famous Iron Guards, eighteen were discharged on surgeon's certificates, four deserted, and eight were unaccounted for. From the Forty-Third Regiment, First Artillery, Battery F, raised in Columbia-Montour Counties, three were released on surgeon's certificates and one deserted. In the Forty-Second Regiment, Company G of Columbia County, one resigned, eighteen were released on surgeon's certificates, seven deserted, and four were given a discharge under a general order. The Eighty-Fourth Regiment, Company D, the noted Hurlay Guards, had two resign and forty-five unaccounted for. Out of the 112th Regiment, Second Artillery, Battery D, raised in Columbia-Montour Counties and headed by Colonel John Freeze, seven were released by general order, one discharged by special order, one was absent, and three were released under surgeon's certificates.

"As to slavery, although some of our neighbors may bemoan the fact, the institution of slavery has a long history in Europe, the colonies, and the United States. Slavery has been legalized by the British Parliament, the American Constitution, British common law cases, and the American Supreme Court. Our country is now fighting a war over legal secession by the Southern states while violating the Constitution by unilaterally creating the state of West Virginia."

Later that afternoon, the Reverend Richard Huntsinger addressed the audience: "Mr. Lincoln studies the Bible. In fact, I have been told that he considers himself to be an expert on the Bible. I do not understand how one who supposedly has studied the Bible in such detail can be so wrong on the issue of slavery. In Genesis chapter 16, it is told that Sarai, the wife of Abram, was barren. Therefore, she delivered unto Abram her handmaiden, an Egyptian whose name was Hagar, so that Hagar might lie with Abram and have children. The Hebrew word used to describe Hagar was *shiphheh*, which translates to 'female slave.' The word for male bondman was *ebed*, which translates to a 'male slave.' These words for male and female slaves are not to be confused with the word *sasir*, which translates to 'a hired servant.' Genesis chapter 24, verse 35 states, 'And Lord hath blessed my master greatly, and he has become great: and he hath given him flocks, and herds, and silver, and gold, and man-servants, and maid-servants, and camels, and asses.' Thus, the Bible clearly indicates that bestowing slaves to Abram and Isaac was a mark of divine favor. Chapter 26, verse 14 names the possessions that belong to Isaac. These include flocks, herds, and a great store of servants. Note, these servants were not nannies, maids, or field hands but were listed as possessions of Isaac. Therefore, he clearly owned them.

"In Exodus, chapter 21, verse 2, it notes, 'if you buy a Hebrew servant, six years he shall serve: and in the seventh he shall go out free for nothing.' This passage clearly talks about a servant or indentured servant that is to go free after seven years. This is in contrast with the manservants and maidservants, which were the possessions of their master. Therefore, the Bible recognizes the possession of slaves as well as that of indentured servants. One is to be freed, and the other is to remain the possession of his master.

"Leviticus, chapter 25, beginning of verse 44, states, 'Both thy bondmen, and thy bondmaids, which thou shall have, shalt be of the heathen that are around; of them shall thee buy bondmen and bondmaids.' Once again, it is clear that these are slaves as they are purchased. Moreover, they are not of the Hebrew faith but are of the persons around them, Gentiles. Verse 45 continues, 'Moreover, of the children of the strangers that do sojourn among you, of them shall ye buy, and of their families that are with you, which they beget in your land: and they shall be your possession. And ye shall take them as an inheritance for your children after you, to inherit them for a possession; they shall be your bondman forever: but over your brethren the children of Israel, ye shall not rule one over the other with rigor.' Therefore, it is apparent that although the ancient Hebrews could be hired servants, the Gentiles could be purchased and held not only for the life of the purchaser but were also to be inherited by their children. This is clear proof that the type of servitude talked about is that of a slave.

"In Numbers, chapter 21, it is noted that the Israelites conquered the Midians. 'And the Lord spoke to Moses saying that he was to take the sum of the prey that was taken, both of man and of beast to divide them between Eleazar, the priest, and the Levites, who were in charge of the tabernacle, named the Children of Israel.' Thus, both man and beast were the spoils of war and were to be possessions of the Israelite people. Clearly, these people taken in battle were to be slaves.

"In Joshua, chapter 9, it is noted that the Gideonites were conquered by Israel. Rather than put them to death, Joshua decided to make them hewers of wood and drawers of water for the congregation. Thus, he spared their lives but made them slaves of the Israelites.

"My friends, it is clear that the Old Testament indicates that the Israelites were warlike people. At times, God commanded them to slay the people they had conquered, but at other times, they were kept as slaves. In addition, Gentiles could be purchased as slaves and to be kept from generation to generation. Clearly, this form of bondage is akin to slavery as it is known today.

"In his work, Politics, Aristotle refers to the word *doulous*, or 'slave.' This word appears in Latin as *servus*, which is the Greek translation of the word *ebed*. These people were bought with money from Gentiles.

"Now, my friends, one may argue that the Old Testament was part of the Old Covenant with the Lord. What then does the New Covenant, or the New Testament, say? If we turn to Galatians, chapter 3, verse 28, it states, 'There is neither Jew nor Greek, there is neither bond nor free, there is neither male nor female; for ye are all one in Christ Jesus.' This passage does not eradicate bondage or slavery but notes that the bondsmen are welcome as Christians.

"In Ephesians chapter 6, verse 5, St. Paul writes, 'Servants, be obedient to them that are your masters according to the flesh, with fear and trembling, in singleness of your heart, as unto Christ.' Therefore, not only does the New Testament recognize the presence of servants or slaves but demands that they be obedient to their masters as they would be obedient unto our Lord. Again, at 1 Timothy chapter 6, St. Paul writes, 'Let as many servants as are under the yoke count their own masters worthy of all honor, let the name of God and His doctrine be not blasphemed. And they that have believing masters, let them not despise them, because they are brethren; but rather do them service, because they are faithful and beloved, partakers of the benefit.' Thus, God commands that slaves honor their masters, especially if their masters are Christian.

"Again, in Titus chapter 2, verse 9, it is said, 'Exhort servants to be obedient unto their own masters, and to please them well in all things; not answering again; not purloining, but showing all good fidelity; that they may adorn the doctrine of God, our Savior in all things.' Thus, St. Paul notes that slaves are to be obedient to their masters in all things and are to strive to please them. In general, the apostles abhorred the abuses of slavery in master-slave relationship, just as they did abuses in the marriage relationship between husband and wife. However, they condemned the wrongful acts in these relationships, not the relationships themselves.

"My friends, before I leave, I would like to discuss two more biblical quotations with you. The first comes from Exodus chapter 21, verse 16. That reads, 'And he that stealeth a man, and selleth him, or if he be found in his hands, he shall surely be put to death.' Well, my friends, abolitionists often site this passage to indicate that slavery is forbidden. However, this passage clearly indicates that if a person stealeth a man and such man is found in his hand, the perpetrator will be put to death. Thus, it is clear that it is the stealing of the man, not his selling, that is the cause of the death sentence. Standing alone, selling one into bondage would not result in a death sentence. Moreover, it is my reading of this verse that the word 'stealeth' means 'to kidnap.' In turn, this relates to the kidnapping of a fellow Jew. Obviously, taking one in battle or purchasing a Gentile or a slave from a Gentile was not forbidden. As such, it is clear to me that this saying does not prohibit slavery.

"Lastly, I would bring to your attention the story of St. Paul, as related in his Epistle to Philemon. In this Epistle, we find St. Paul in prison. By some means, a slave named Onesimus, belonged to Philemon, was in prison with Paul and helping him. Although it is obvious that Paul was quite fond of Onesimus, he returned him to his master, Philemon. Surely, St. Paul could have told Onesimus that slavery was wrong and that he was free. He could have refused to return him to Philemon, or he could have upbraided Philemon for holding the slave. However, he did not do this. He knew that Onesimus was a slave and he returned him to his master.

"None other than the head of the Reformation and noted biblical scholar Martin Luther concluded that the writer of Philemon did not in any way change the social status or position of Onesimus.

"There are many other parts of the Old and New Testaments that speak of bondmen or slaves. As we have seen, there are sections that speak to the relationship between the slave and the master. There are no parts of the Bible that prohibit or condemn slavery. The ancient Jews practiced slavery, and during the time of Jesus, slaves were still held. However, neither Jesus nor any of the persons who wrote the scriptures condemned that institution.

"The Bible even endorses succession! At 3 Kings 12 we see that the king of Israel, Rehoboam, was unjust, and God turned away from him. As a result, Jeroboam led the ten northern tribes to succeed from the confederation. Rehoboam became enraged and began to form an army to make war on Jeroboam. But the Lord sent Semeias to tell Rehoboam not to make war on Jeroboam.

"Today, our king, ol' Abe, is not only unjust, but he went one step further than Reboboam and made war on the succeeding states. Thus, he has done what the Lord forbade Rehoboam from doing. He has compounded his sin of tyranny by waging war."

Later in the afternoon, a letter from George W. Howell, a soldier from Columbia County then serving in Virginia, was read:

> Uncle Sam will have to quit having wite men shot for the sake of freeing a few infernal niggars before he gets me to pick up a musket again. Now I for my part dont believe in having 100 white killed to free one or two slaves nor I don't care about shooting a rebille for to take his Slaves from him. for, I believe they have a rite to hold them and old abe, I think was out of place when he issued his useless proclamation. now, I wouldnt mind playing soldier if it was not for the purpose

of freeing the negro, and then have him made our
superiors. if old abe has command of the shanty
a few years laonger. the negor respect more than
the white man . . .

This letter, along with the previously given statistics
regarding local soldiers who had one way or the other left
the service by desertion or by shirking responsibility with a
surgeon's certificate, was given as proof that locals were indeed
very patriotic when it came to saving the Union. However,
their enthusiasm waned when the purpose of the war was
changed from saving the Union to freeing the slaves.

As the day wore on, more reasonable people were heard.
Local men believed that they would be playing into the hands
of the union troops fighting them in a pitch battle. Obviously,
the troops were specifically trained for this type of warfare and,
if given time, could bring their artillery to bear. Instead, it was
concluded that five leaders would be chosen to lead five groups
of men who would engage in hit-and-run tactics should the
Union troops move north and begin burning barns or crops,
murdering the local citizenry, or raping the womenfolk.

For all the talk in engaging Union troops en masse or
by use of guerilla tactics, the local men were taken totally
unaware during the early morning raid in August. The raids
were conducted without a shot being fired and without any
fatalities or severe injuries.

Chapter VI

PRISON

When the prisoners were loaded into a cattle car at the Lackawanna & Bloomsburg Rail Road in Bloomsburg, Jacob Saddler quickly went to the rear and took a seat in the corner. He felt he would have some semblance of privacy. He was to find out this was not a good location. During the long trip, men had to relieve themselves, and urinating out the slats in the back of the cattle car was the best method possible. Jacob migrated to the front of the car and sat on the floor. As the car swayed to and fro, Jacob became mesmerized by the clicking of the rails. He was aware that each click took him farther away from his home and his beloved Katherine. The train traveled southward through the rolling hills and farmland. Eventually, it broke into a section with hills on the left and a wide river on the right. The prisoners correctly deduced that this was the Susquehanna River. As night fell, Jacob was able to get a little sleep. Around 2:00 a.m., the prisoners could see a rather large city in front of them. They had arrived in Harrisburg. It was the general opinion that this is where their trials would be held. It would take an entire day for relatives to travel by buggy from Columbia County down to Harrisburg, have a visit, and return.

Much to the surprise of the prisoners, they were unloaded from the cattle car, marched a short distance, and placed in yet another cattle car. The train slowly moved out of the station, and the prisoners found themselves again heading south with the Susquehanna River on the right. The train eventually moved away from the river and through York County. In the early light, Jacob could see what appeared to be rather ramshackle barns. He was informed by some of the prisoners that these were actually tobacco sheds, and the missing slats on the side were intentional, as they let air through to cure the tobacco. Jacob could not help but smile. He knew that one of his ancestors had been a tobacconist and would have immediately recognized the usefulness of such sheds. He mused that such information was lost from generation to generation but that each generation picked up new information that would be more useful to them.

Eventually, an even larger city loomed on the horizon. They arrived in Philadelphia at 7:00 a.m. on September 1. The prisoners were marched from Market Street to the corner of Fifth and Buttonwood, where they were placed in the fifth floor of a filthy building. Other floors of the building were used to temporarily house deserters, draft dodgers, and prisoners of war. The men were given tin cups of soup with some bread and meat. The next morning, they were marched to the Arch Street Wharf, where they were to board the steamer *Raybold*.

Before the ship arrived, the officer in charge turned the prisoners over to a sergeant for a roll call. Each man was told that when he heard his name, he was to yell "here" and to step forward. The men were lined up, and the sergeant began the roll call.

Daniel McHenry	Elias McHenry	Joseph Coleman
Mathias Kline	Abraham Kline	Samuel Coleman
Joseph Coleman	Charles Coleman	John Lemons
Silas Benjamin	Samuel Appleman	William Appleman
Reuben Appleman	Thomas Appleman	James McHenry
Jacob Saddler	Dyer Chapin	Elias McHenry
Samuel Kline	John Rantz	William Roberts
John York	Henry Hurliman	George Hurliman
John Stiles	Hiram Everett	Scott Collett
Benjamin Collett	Joseph Van Sickle	Rohr McHenry
John Karns	John C. Karns	Montgomery Cole
Russell McHenry	James Evans	Jonathan Steele
H. H. Hurliman	William Hurlyman	Valentine Fell
John Davis	Armillis Davis	Samuel McHenry
M. D. Appleman	John Baker	Abram Hartman

When the roll call ended, the soldiers were astounded. One man remained standing in his original place. There were forty-five names on the list, and forty-five men had stepped forward, but still, one remained in place. A recount was done, but they still had an extra man. The guards found that the additional man was Silas McHenry. Although there were a number of McHenrys on the list, Silas was not included. They didn't know what to do. Fortunately, the officer was more decisive. If the man was not on the list, he was not under their jurisdiction and had to be released. If indeed he was to be charged with something, he could always be rearrested. Thus, Silas McHenry was released. The provost marshal concluded that he should be placed on a train with the next group of wounded soldiers headed to northeastern Pennsylvania. A hasty collection was taken among the prisoners, and he was given a few dollars. Wherever he landed, he could take a train to Bloomsburg or telegraph relatives to come and pick him up.

Of the forty-five prisoners who boarded the steamer, thirty-seven were listed as farmers. In addition, there were three carpenters, two merchants, one innkeeper, one blacksmith, and one wheelwright. The prisoners ranged in age from eighteen (Jacob Saddler) to sixty-eight, (Joseph Coleman). Mr. Coleman was a veteran of the War of 1812 and was obviously too old to serve in the military during the Civil War. John Rantz, age sixty, was to emerge as the prisoners' leader and spokesman. John Karns, age twenty-three, had served honorably for nine months. Armillis Davis had been drafted while on a trip out west and had been only recently notified of his draft status.

After a short but seemingly endless trip on the Delaware River, the prisoners disembarked and were forced to march to a starburst-shaped structure. They were incarcerated in Fort Mifflin, just outside Philadelphia.

None of the prisoners knew the history of Fort Mifflin and, most likely, could not have cared less. In 1771, Captain John Motresor, of the British Army, began building what was then known as Mud Island Fort on the banks of the Delaware River. This fort, along with another fort on the distant bank, controlled access to Philadelphia. The fort was not completed until 1776, under the auspices of the rebel colony of Pennsylvania.

In 1777, Washington was defeated at the Battle of Brandywine and began a slow retreat to Valley Forge. In those days, it was not customary to wage war in wintertime, but British forces were hot on the trail of Washington and his troops. The British had 250 ships and two thousand troops that they wanted to land and pursue Washington. If they were able to catch him, they would be able to defeat his army before the onset of winter. However, the Mud Island Fort was manned by 400 to 450 patriots and stood in the way of British troops. The 250 British ships lined up and bombarded the patriots at Mud Island Fort. This bombardment continued from October 1777 through mid-November. It is estimated that approximately ten thousand cannon shots were launched. Most of the fort was reduced to rubble and eighty-five of the defenders were killed before surrendering on November 15, 1777. By then, it was too late for the British to pursue Washington. Mud Island was later named Fort Mifflin, the fort that saved America. In his memoirs, General Washington noted its importance and of his need to safely set up a winter camp. Ironically, the British officer in charge of the besieging the fort was none other than Captain John Motresor, who had designed it. In 1795, the ruins were rebuilt under the direction of Pierre L'Enfant, who planned the young nation's capital.

Had the prisoners known the history of the fort, they would have found it ironic. They would have felt that the freedoms their forefathers had fought and died for were now being denied to them as they were now incarcerated in one of the bastions of that fight for liberty.

In all, approximately thirteen thousand Northern civilians were detained by the Union military. In addition to Fort Mifflin, these civilians were to be housed in Fort Lafayette, New York; Fort Warren, Massachusetts; Fort McHenry, Maryland; and Fort Monroe, Virginia.

The prisoners were marched over the footbridge covering the moat that surrounded the fort. At this point, they had been marched well over twenty miles in two days. Immediately upon entering the front gate, the prisoners were directed to the right and into a tunnel. The first bombproof or casement on the left was the largest and held numerous Confederate prisoners of war. Casements 2, 3, and 4 were reserved for civilian prisoners, and the men from Columbia County were placed in bombproof 3. Bombproofs were underground shelters with a thick covering of stone and sod over the roof meant to protect people and ammunition from enemy artillery.

This bombproof was fifty-four feet long and approximately nineteen feet wide. Between three to four feet up the sidewall, the bricks began to form an arch or dome, thus cutting down further on the amount of space available. Pieces of wood left over from construction were placed on the ground, and boards were placed over the blocks to form beds. Not all of the fifty-four-foot room was available for beds, as there was a small stove near the outer wall, and a slop bucket was placed near the entrance each night. Therefore, most prisoners had a twenty-four-inch wide space in which to sleep. Many of the men found it was impossible for three men to sleep shoulder to shoulder. Usually, one would sleep in the opposite direction, or one or two of the men would sleep in a position where they were virtually sitting up. Due to the cold and dampness, the older men were placed closer to the fire near the outer wall. The two youngest men, Jacob Saddler and William Hurlyman, age nineteen, were placed nearest the door. The most disagreeable guard, Corporal Frank Brown, was in charge of the prisoners. He assigned William and Jacob to empty the slop bucket. This was a barrel with the top cut off and holes drilled near the top to accommodate handles. Once or twice per day, they were given a board to place through the holes at each end of the bucket. Under guard, they had to lift the bucket on their shoulders and carefully carry it out of the tunnel leading from the casements through the main gate and out to the moat that surrounded the fort. In that moat, which the prisoners called a lagoon, they emptied the slop bucket. The prisoners were required to draw their drinking water from this same lagoon, or moat, that carried the prisoners' waste. If the water was not boiled, the prisoners were subject to dysentery and other such diseases.

The prisoners were given no bedding, except for one blanket per prisoner. Most of the prisoners used this blanket to cover themselves at night; some rolled it up and used it for a pillow. Each man received one loaf of bread per day. The morning meal consisted of a slice of boiled pork or beef and a tin of coffee. Dinner consisted of bean or pea soup with meat occasionally substituted for the vegetables. They were given only a tin of coffee at night. Occasionally, they would receive boiled potato soup for dinner. Sometimes meat was not provided, and sometimes it was rancid. The prisoners were given half a candle for the entire room per day. However, they were allowed to purchase additional candles and food from the guards at exorbitant rates. After several weeks, General Couch visited the men. He ordered that each man be given a second blanket and that they all be given an exercise period in the yard twice per week. It was near the end of October before the extra blankets arrived, and the men were allotted only two exercise periods during their entire confinement.

Corporal Brown took a particular dislike to Jacob. Perhaps this was because he was the youngest prisoner or because he was a Quaker. Either way, he seemed the most vulnerable of the prisoners. Corporal Brown would often push Jacob or try to trip him as he walked past. Brown would refer to Jacob as "Quaker Boy" and would often mock him by using the words "thee" or "thy."

A few days after their arrival, Corporal Brown told Jacob that he was to report to the officer in charge of the prison guards, Captain Michael Kelly. Brown let on that Jacob must have done something terribly wrong and that he was in a good deal of trouble. Needless to say, Jacob was very nervous when he was escorted to Captain Kelly's quarters.

Upon entering Captain Kelly's quarters, Jacob was told to take a seat. Kelly began, "I'll be blunt and come to the point. I need an aide to clean my quarters twice a week and was wondering if you would be interested in the job. It will get you out of that dungeon and provide you with a healthier atmosphere, at least on a temporary basis." As it turned out, Jacob was to spend most of this time talking with Captain Kelly rather than cleaning his quarters. The captain explained that he had been born in a small town of Keadue in County Roscommon, Ireland, in 1840. He was but five years old when the potato crops failed. He noted that his family was one of numerous tenant farmers and that they were hit particularly hard by the failure of the potato crop. Basically, as tenant farmers, they were allotted a one-third acre of land to grow potatoes to sustain themselves. His mother and father both worked as farmers for the landlord and produced the cash crops of vegetables and grain that were not for their consumption but for sale in England and Scotland. In order to avoid starvation, his father would walk several miles to the town of Boyle, where he received a ration of soup from a kitchen run by the Quakers. For this reason, the captain credited Quakers with saving his family. He said his father could have gone into one of the workhouses. However, to do so, the family would have had to give up their one-third acre. They were not willing to do this. Moreover, admission to a workhouse meant that they would be in close contact with people dying from dysentery, cholera, and other contagious diseases. The small amount of gruel that they would have received from the workhouse would not have made up for the calories expended in the work they were required to do. In many instances, this work was building roads. By and large, such roads were not needed and did not go anywhere. Hence, they were known as "roads to nowhere." One of the alternatives was to get food from the "soupers." In exchange, they would have been required to give up their Catholic religion and to convert to the Anglican faith. Like most rural Catholics at the time, they would rather starve than to give up their religion.

During these sessions in the captain's quarters, Jacob learned about the original invasion of Ireland by Strongbow in the twelfth century. He was told how many of the English conquerors settled in Ireland and eventually became part of the Irish culture. For a long period, many of the British forces were contained within the pale around Dublin. It was considered foolish for them to go unescorted out of the pale into the Irish countryside. Thus, doing something foolish or outlandish became known as going "beyond the pale."

Jacob learned that in the early seventeenth century, the Spanish landed forces at Kinsale. The leaders of the various Irish clans, including the powerful clans of Ulster, moved southward to aid the Spanish. They were met and defeated by the English during the Battle of Kinsale. This broke the Irish clans. As a result, most of the lords of the north fled to the continent. This was known as the Flight of the Earls. More importantly, it left a power vacuum in Northern Ireland. The British masters decided to fill this vacuum by forcibly moving mostly Scotch Presbyterians into Northern Ireland. This became known as The Plantations of Ireland and approximately a half-million acres were ceded to the newcomers.

In the mid-seventeenth century, Lord Oliver Cromwell invaded Ireland and engaged in mass destruction, murder, and mayhem. Under the Cromwellian policy of "to hell or Connaught," many Irish were killed or driven from the north to the bare western province of Connaught. This further opened millions of acres of land that were, in turn, settled by more Scotch Presbyterians. This plantation of Presbyterians and a few Anglicans became a bone of contention between the remaining Irish and British elements.

Under the Treaty of Limerick, the Irish were to retain the rights they had prior to the rebellion. However, what they received were the Penal Laws. In brief, these laws severely restricted the practice of the Catholic religion and a Catholic's right to land ownership. The result was that the vast majority of rural Irish-Catholics were kept in a condition of perpetual poverty. The victory of William of Orange at the Battle of the Boyne resulted in an Anglican-English monarchy in perpetuity.

Captain Kelly was fond of saying that God had created the failure of the potato crop, but the British government, under Charles Trevelyan, had created the famine. He noted that that potato famine was widespread through Europe but that most monarchs or local royalty purchased corn or other grains on the open market to feed their peasants. However, in Ireland, many of the landlords were absentee landlords and were actually grateful to have their Irish peasants starve. The British government was loath to provide any food for the starving Irish, as this was against free-market principles. When the burden of caring for the sick and starving was removed from the government and placed on the local landlords, many of them decided to solve this problem by paying their peasants to emigrate. Thus, thousands of peasants were placed on "coffin ships" and transported to Canada and the United States.

Captain Kelly noted that conditions were such that his mother, Marie, pretended to take her share of food but actually split it among his father, William; his sister, Colleen; and himself. As a result, Marie eventually starved. His sister, Colleen, developed cholera and died. William was distraught. He saw no future in Ireland and took up his landlord's offer of passage to the United States.

In 1848, William took his son, Michael, then age eight, on the long journey to New York. William was fortunate enough to land a job as a bartender but, unfortunately, took up the drink. However, he did save enough money to see that Michael was educated by the Jesuits. Michael took the top prize in his class for reading, writing, and speaking in English. On the side, his father made sure that he also kept up with his Irish.

When war broke out in 1861, Michael was twenty-one years old and volunteered his services to save the Union. As a result of his education and letters of recommendation from the clergy and local politicians, he was granted a commission as a lieutenant.

Captain Kelly's reason for wanting to join the army to help save the Union, he said, was that he was grateful to his adopted country and felt although they lived in poor circumstances in New York City, America had saved his and his father's life. He felt that in Ireland the British had regarded the Irish as subhuman and treated them accordingly. He noted that during the wars of the seventeenth century, many English soldiers had returned home and stated that the Irish actually had tails, similar to monkeys. Perhaps it was easier for the English forces to kill the Irish if they considered them to be subhuman, Captain Kelly speculated.

During their conversations, Jacob learned that Captain Kelly was not in favor of the emancipation of the slaves. Kelly had seen some slaves on the of Philadelphia docks and during his brief campaign in Maryland. He considered them uneducated and rather dull people who, by their physique, were best suited for laboring positions. In short, he considered them inferior to the white race.

The irony of the English view of the Irish and Captain Kelly's view of Negroes was not lost on Jacob. Because Kelly was his benefactor, Jacob never brought up the issue.

During their various meetings, Captain Kelly quizzed Jacob on religion of the Society of Friends or Quakers. Although Kelly found the Quakers to be very religious, friendly, and industrious, he felt they did not realize the necessity of fighting for one's country or one's religion. He reasoned that if everyone were to take this tact, the Moors would have overrun Europe and the Christian religion, and there would be no hope for the Irish. Kelly noted that when Confederate troops invaded the North during the Battle of Gettysburg, many of the Quakers from that area and from York and Lancaster counties actually volunteered to take up arms and defend the Union.

Jacob admitted that he had heard it was true, saying it was up to each Quaker to follow his individual conscience.

Kelly was interested in knowing how the Quaker community would react to having some of their brethren take up arms and kill rebels.

Jacob said that just as the decision to take up arms was up to each Quaker, each Quaker's reaction to their brethren fighting was also a matter of individual conscience. Some Quakers might be able to abide such activities while others might shun their brethren. Therefore, the problem lay not with each individual Quaker but with each meetinghouse where opinions might be divided.

Captain Kelly wanted to know whether Jacob would take up arms if the religion of the Friends or the Christian religion as a whole was threatened. Jacob said he did not believe he could take up arms or intentionally do harm to his fellow humans under any circumstance. Kelly scoffed at this, noting that under the proper circumstances, it was not only allowable but mandatory that Christians take up arms in defense of Christianity or a Christian nation.

Without thinking, Jacob blurted out, "So your motto is 'in the name of the Prince of Peace, kill!'"

Kelly wheeled around and glared at Jacob. Jacob's face reddened, and he wondered if he had gone too far and ruined their friendship. Eventually, Kelly's tone softened and he said, "I really never thought of it in those terms." He told Jacob if everyone were a pacifist, it would be the death knell of Christianity.

The two of them often discussed this topic. Jacob noted that Jesus was known as the Prince of Peace, that the meek would inherit the earth. He called Jesus a pacifist and argued that even when his own life was threatened, he refused to take up arms or to become violent. Therefore, Jacob said, to truly follow Christ meant that one should be nonviolent too.

Captain Kelly granted these points but argued that at one point in the Gospels, Jesus checked his disciples to make sure that each one had a sword (Luke 22:36-38). If they did not have a sword, they were to go out and purchase one. He noted that Jesus's followers were armed, as one of his disciples had cut off the ear of a Roman soldier at the Garden of Gethsemane. He also noted that Jesus had stated that he did not come to bring peace, but to bring a sword (Matthew 10:34). Again, in Luke 12:51, Jesus denies that he has come to bring peace. Jacob argued that it was God who was to wield a sword, not man.

Jacob was at a loss as to whether or not to broach the subject of Corporal Brown's increasing harassment. At one point, Captain Kelly had let it slip that Brown had twice been promoted to sergeant and twice broken back to corporal due to being drunk on duty. Jacob deduced that Brown was not Captain Kelly's favorite trooper. His visits with Captain

Kelly not only resulted in a break from the horrid conditions in the bombproof, but also often resulted in presents of root beer, sarsaparilla, and pastries. Jacob had become quite fond of his visits with Captain Kelly and decided not to mention harassment by Corporal Brown for fear of ruining the relationship.

Due to the cramped quarters and filthy conditions, tempers often flared, resulting in fights among the prisoners. Whenever a fight broke out, Jacob moved to a far corner. Eventually, John Rantz, the de facto leader of the prisoners in casement 3, convinced the prisoners that they must hold their tempers. He argued that the fellow prisoners were not the enemy; the Lincoln administration and the guards were their enemy.

Chapter VII

POLITICS AND DEATH

During their stay at Fort Mifflin, the prisoners were denied visitors, as well as their right to counsel. Colonel Wellington H. Ent of Columbia County did get to visit the prisoners for a short period. Ent was from Lightstreet and had joined the original Iron Guards as a first lieutenant. He proved his mettle in the battles of South Mountain and Antietam Creek and rose quickly through the ranks. Due to bravery during the Battle of the Wilderness, he was promoted to brigadier general. Despite his status, he was unable to ascertain the nature of the charges against the men. He knew some of them had donated money for draft replacements and that some had sons serving in the military.

The prisoners were allowed to receive packages. Once the folks at home learned of the destination of their loved ones, they began sending packages of clothing and nonperishable food items. Gifts of union suits and woolen socks were particularly welcome. There would be the occasional tin of meat or vegetables; homemade cookies were particularly welcomed. Bakery items, such as pies and cakes, often did not survive the journey. Even if they did, they often did not make it through the guard's quarters where packages were inspected.

The arrival of the first pair of dice caused a sensation. Life within the bombproofs was very boring, and this allowed them to pass time by gambling. But it often resulted in increased violence. Eventually, the first deck of playing cards made its way into the casements. The first decks were met with ambivalence. The prisoners were more than glad to receive the cards so they could engage in a whole new round of betting activities. It was not lost on them that the decks were "Union cards." The cards often had patriotic or militaristic pictures on the face. They were often quickly disfigured. After all, it made no difference so long as the back of the cards gave no indication of their face value. America was sometimes portrayed as Miss Liberty. Although pictures of Miss Liberty were not marred, snide comments were made about her chastity, or lack thereof.

Jacob did not take part in the games of chance but spent his time working for Captain Kelly. He also spent time reading a Bible that had been provided by Kelly.

At the end of his second week of confinement, Jacob received a small package by mail. It was from Katherine. She had asked Colonel Freeze for the address. He gave it reluctantly. His own early letters had been returned. Katherine's package was a test. If Jacob received it, he could use the enclosed writing paper to respond.

Jacob was elated. Many prisoners were still suspicious of him. His talks with Captain Kelly were helpful. But Kelly was, after all, the head jailer, so Jacob was limited as to what he could say. Katherine's package contained a letter. The letter contained questions. How was he being treated? Was he getting enough to eat? Was there anything he needed?

Jacob did not want to be too critical. He feared the guards might not let such a letter go through. In addition, he did not want to upset his beloved Kathy. He responded that the prisoners all received three meals per day. They were adequate, but the variety of food was limited. The guards were not friendly, but only one went out of his way to bother Jacob.

There was always a shove, a slap, an attempted trip, or a snide comment. He hated to ask Katherine for anything.

Jacob finally swallowed his pride and responded. The cell was damp, and some spare clothing would be most appreciated.

Katherine was delighted to receive his letter. A line of communication had been opened. She worked part-time in her father's dry-goods store. It was a simple matter to pick out a pair of pants and socks, a shirt, and union suit. She placed the appropriate amount of money in the till. It was just another routine sale as far as the inventory was concerned.

The second package was much larger. The clothing was a bit large for him, as Jacob had lost weight. He found oatmeal cookies and ginger snaps cleverly folded in the clothing. They were a most welcome surprise. Jacob was baffled by the enclosed letter.

She had always followed her father's support of the war effort. Katherine wrote that she had seen far too many men return with missing arms or legs. One poor fellow was especially pitiful. He had taken a Minie-ball through his upper jaw. The entry wound on the right was still visible. Much worse, the left side of his face was disfigured by the exit wound. There was still a one-inch hole the surgeons could not close. Part of his upper jaw and gums were visible. The teeth had been blown away, and he was left with a painful open wound that was subject to infection and resulted in uncontrolled drooling. The man would never marry. Perhaps he could work as a farmhand. Any position that required dealing with the public was out of the question. Katherine also was aware that she would not see men suffering from battle fatigue, those whose minds had hidden in a dark place, never again to see the light of polite society. The lucky ones would be shielded from the public by family members. The less lucky would be sent to insane asylums.

His beloved still longed for the reunion of the states and abolition of slavery. However, she believed the cost was too high. Wars always ended with a treaty. Why in God's name could not reasonable men agree on a resolution before the war? She felt the killing and maiming had to cease immediately. There was no cause that should move one man to take up arms against his fellow man.

Jacob was stunned but glad to hear of the change. Perhaps if they were to marry, she would join the Society of Friends.

It was early Tuesday, just past midnight, when Corporal Brown quietly opened the cell door. He gently shook Jacob awake and made a motion that he should be quiet and come with him. Jacob rolled out of bed and quickly put on his shoes. He wondered what particular torture the corporal had in mind at this hour. Brown locked the casement door behind them and proceeded down the tunnel. He locked the outer door and picked up a lantern from a nearby table. They continued across the compound to the blacksmith shop. Corporal Brown rolled back the door of the blacksmith shop and told Jacob to proceed to the far left-hand corner. Jacob did so gingerly, as it was quite dark, and he did not want to fall. On reaching the corner, he turned around. Instantly, Corporal Brown was upon him. Jacob acted instinctively. He pushed Brown away. Normally, a person would have taken one or two steps backward. As usual, Brown was drunk. He fell backward, and his head hit the base of the blacksmith's hearth with a sickening thud.

For several seconds, Jacob stood there quaking in terror. In a dimly lit room, he could barely make out something unusual about Brown's head. Eventually, he stepped over the body and knelt down. To his horror, what he had seen was a small river of blood trickling on the floor. The odor of blood was mixed with the odor of whiskey; Brown's hip flask had broken when he fell. Jacob delicately touched Brown's throat, but no pulse was detected. He bent over but could hear no heartbeat. He moved the lantern over and saw that Brown's eyes were fixed.

Jacob shuddered in horror as he realized he had killed Brown. Clearly, he had not meant to do so. His reaction had been instinctive and involuntary. He realized that some of the blood had reached his shoe and jumped back in horror. His mind was racing; he did not know what to do. At first, he thought he might turn himself in and hope that Captain Kelly would intervene and treat him leniently.

However, he knew the vindictiveness of the guards and decided against it. He was about to turn off the lantern, but he thought better of it. If the death was to be considered an accident, the natural course of events would be that the lantern would be left behind to burn out. Therefore, he simply turned it down a few notches so as to avoid detection. He slipped the keys off of Brown's belt and walked over to the door. He looked outside. There were no guards in sight.

Jacob quickly crossed the compound. He made sure to walk quickly, but not run. He did not hold the keys by the key chain but held all of them in his hands so they would not make noise. There were a half-dozen keys on the ring, and he had to go through several before he found the one to open the main door. He then proceeded to casement 3 and again went through the keys until he found the proper one. Jacob quietly opened the door a little bit. He proceeded back through the tunnel and outside. Jacob put the keys on the guard's desk, closed the main door, went back to the casement, and closed the door behind him.

Jacob did not sleep that night. He worried that he would be found out and what would happen as a result. Although several men got up to use the slop bucket during the night, none of them touched the door. After all, it was assumed the door was locked, and there was no reason to try to open it.

The blacksmith's apprentice found Brown's body between five and six in the morning when he reported for work. Word of Brown's death quickly spread among the troopers and eventually filtered down to the prisoners.

There was not a lot of mourning for Brown among his fellow soldiers, as he had always been mean-spirited. The reaction of the prisoners was just short of elation.

It just happened that Jacob was scheduled to meet with Captain Kelly that morning. The captain noted that Jacob looked tired. Kelly stated that inquiries would be made. The assumption was that Brown had left his post to drink, as was his custom. It appeared that in his drunken state he had slipped and fallen. Likely, the death would be ruled an accident.

Brown's replacement wasn't exactly Santa Claus. But then again, he was a guard and was not expected to be kind to the prisoners. Still, he was a vast improvement over the surly and obnoxious Brown. Jacob's life continued to be one of three meals a day, emptying the slop buckets, and meeting with Captain Kelly.

Katherine did not know of the death of Corporal Brown. She did notice a change in Jacob's letters. He could not be specific, but he noted that a brief act of violence had resulted in a vast improvement of his circumstances. He noted that in the Old Testament, God had approved of war and even of the slaughter of women and children. Nations resorted to violence to solve their differences. Indeed, their nation was in the midst of that process. It now appeared the Union would be victorious. The nation would again be united and slavery abolished. He now believed that violence applied in defense of a good cause was justified. Katherine felt his turnaround was remarkable. She would never know the specifics of his situation.

While the prisoners bided their time in Fort Mifflin awaiting a possible legal solution to their dilemma, a political movement was underway to free the prisoners. It was generally known that various members of the Lincoln administration could be bribed to release an occasional prisoner of war. However, the money needed to release 45 political prisoners made a mass bribe out of the question.

Senator Charles Buckalew led the political maneuverings. As his right-hand man, he chose Colonel John Freeze. He considered Freeze to be the best attorney in the area. The senator also felt Freeze would be a calming influence should he become angry. At one point, they attempted to enlist the cooperation of General George McClellan. For his part, McClellan was aware of criticism that he was sympathetic to the Confederate cause. Thus, he demurred.

On a Friday in mid-October, Senator Buckalew and Colonel Freeze approached General Couch in his headquarters at Chambersburg, Pennsylvania. Buckalew entered the room first, taking the chair near the window to Couch's left. Behind Couch were portraits of President Lincoln and Secretary of War Stanton. The senator got right to the point. He asked that the prisoners be released and noted none of them had resisted arrest and none were draft dodgers or deserters. He pointed out there was no record of any defendant engaged in insurrection.

Buckalew noted that the civilian federal courts were in operation and said the prisoners should be tried therein. General Couch stated he did not know the specifics of any planned trials and that he would approach Washington on how to proceed. Colonel Freeze raised the issue of bail for the prisoners. General Couch bluntly refused to grant any bail.

Senator Buckalew concluded such bond was of no use if the prisoners were to be tried by a military tribunal, which, he added, would be illegal. Couch responded that, were that the case, denial of bail was well-founded. Buckalew became uneasy.

Colonel Freeze said he feared the prisoners were being ill-treated and denied the right of counsel. General Couch replied the prisoners were allowed the right of counsel and that rumors the men were miserably housed and poorly fed were totally untrue.

Buckalew noted Freeze's face turned red with anger. He raised his voice, contending that he and various attorneys had attempted to contact the prisoners but were rebuffed. Buckalew smiled, thinking, "So this is the man I brought along to keep me calm."

Senator Buckalew was calmer. He asked General Couch if he was sure the prisoners were well-treated and well-fed. General Couch replied that, to the best of his knowledge, this was true. Actually, Couch had little knowledge of the day-to-day conditions of the prisoners. Now Buckalew began to stew. He had recently been approached by numerous constituents who were angry about the recent death of one of the prisoners. He then asked the general if he could answer a question for him. The general nodded. Buckalew gritted his teeth and noted that only days prior to the meeting, a prisoner named William Roberts had died. The most likely cause of his death was dysentery, caused by polluted water. "How could this be if the prisoners are well-housed and well-fed?" He noted Couch turned crimson and squirmed in his chair. The general nodded to his aide, who immediately left the room to check on the situation. All General Couch could say was that he was not aware of this development

Buckalew was amazed. How could the general come to a meeting with a United States senator so unprepared? Was the general lying or just stupid? Either way, the general had learned he was not addressing two privates cowering in their boots. The senator now felt he was in charge, and he would press his advantage.

Senator Buckalew asked the general to release some of the prisoners, noting that if additional deaths followed, General Couch might well have an insurrection on his hands. He further threatened that if some action were not taken, he would contact General Couch's superior, Simon Cameron, and even contact the president. Couch became restless. He was on bad terms with Cameron. He knew Cameron's demeanor. This meant that if he did not release any prisoners, Cameron would do so just to show that Couch had used poor judgment.

General Couch promised he would order the immediate release of any prisoner found to be ill. He further ordered his subordinate, Colonel Sullivan Meredith, to review the charges against the remaining prisoners. He predicted, in all likelihood, only five to seven prisoners would actually stand trial. After the review, it was recommended that twenty-one prisoners be released. Captain Francis Wessels, the judge advocate in charge of the prosecution, objected, and Couch delayed the release of additional prisoners.

Prisoners Elias McHenry, age forty-seven; H. H. Hurliman, age forty-nine; James Evans, age fifty-three; and Reuben Appleman, age twenty-five, were deemed to be sick and released. Joseph Coleman, age sixty-eight, a veteran of the War of 1812, was also released. Coleman, McHenry, and Hurliman spent forty-nine days in captivity, and Evans and Appleman fifty-two days. On the fifty-third day, Samuel Coleman, Charles Coleman, Silas Benjamin, Samuel Appleman, John Karns,

Montgomery Cole, William Hurlyman, John Davis, Samuel McHenry, M. D. Appleman, and John Baker were released. Rohr McHenry was released after two months. Various other prisoners would be acquitted and would be released in four months or shortly thereafter.

As Senator Buckalew noted to General Couch, William Roberts had been released by a higher power. Although all the prisoners were to become local heroes, only Mr. Roberts was to become a martyr. In his honor, a poem was written:

> Sleep on, old friend, thy sleep is dreamless.
> No midnight raids disturb thee now.
> To thee the Tyrants' shafts are aimless,
> He's stuck his last, though fatal blow.
>
> While guided by some "loyal" minions,
> They reach thy distant cabin doors;
> In for thine honest hearts opinion,
> Thee from thy wife and children tore.
>
> With tottering steps we saw thee going,
> And marked by walking in the row;
> Thine agent form 'twas easy knowing,
> Thy locks and beard like fleecy snow.
>
> With cool haste they urged thee onward,
> Yes, onward to the filthy gaol;
> From which thy friends soon carried homeward,
> Thy body emptied of its soul.

Though gone the patriot heart will cherish,
Each recollection of thy name;
And from the record shall not perish,
For thou shalt have historic fame.

We leave thee in silent slumber;
Our feeble pen can do no more,
Then mention thee among the member,
The murder now left 44.

A rumor hit the compound. Trials were to begin in Harrisburg.

Chapter VIII

THE TRIAL

Rumors of impending trials multiplied daily. The remaining twenty-four prisoners were awakened early one morning near the end of October. Each man was given four pieces of twine. They were ordered to roll their belongings in their blanket and secure the roll with the twine. What property was left could be discarded or inventoried and kept for them.

Jacob was called to Captain Kelly's quarters for the last time. The captain apologized that he would not be there to see Jacob leave. Kelly had just finished a double shift as duty officer and was dog-tired.

The captain thanked Jacob for their conversations, and Jacob thanked the captain for his kindness and food. Kelly asked Jacob for a last favor. Would he help him take off his boots? Jacob quickly assented. He faced away from Kelly, straddling his left leg. With the toe of the boot in his left hand and the heel in the right, he gave a mighty heave. For an instant, nothing moved. Kelly gave him a push from behind, and slowly the boot gave way. The process was repeated with the right foot.

Both men stood, shook hands, and wished each other well. As Jacob left, he felt it odd that his last memory of Kelly would be of him standing in full uniform but without his boots.

Jacob made it back to the bombproof just as the men assembled into four columns and six lines. They retraced their path to Philadelphia. This time, they were placed in a regular coach for the trip to Harrisburg. The men were disbursed throughout the coach so as to minimize contact. Fully armed soldiers were stationed fore and aft.

Jacob was again mesmerized by the swaying of the train and the clicking of the rails. This time he did not concentrate on his future but on the death of Corporal Brown. Jacob's reflexive violent act had killed Brown. Yet it had solved the problem of constant harassment. Jacob had originally thought that by being passive and kind Brown would see his goodness and would eventually treat him fairly. However, the nicer he was, the more intolerable Brown became. Jacob was riveted on the fact that violence, rather than kindness, had liberated him from Brown's torment. He now wished he had been able to vanquish his tormentors during his school years with force. How was the Union going to survive? By force! This was how nations solve their problems. He decided that appropriately selected and applied force would be of better use than pacifism in handling such problems.

Once in Harrisburg, the prisoners were placed several men to a cell with bunks and decent food. Even better, there was an outhouse rather than a slop bucket. During the journey, Jacob became fidgety and stuck his hands into his pockets. He felt a strange object and pulled it out. It was a $10 gold piece. For a moment, he was puzzled, as he knew he had no money on him. Where did this come from? There could be but one source—Captain Kelly. He remembered the shove Kelly had given him while he was removing the captain's boots. It must have been inserted then. Jacob slipped the coin into a tear in the armpit of his jacket. He slumped in his seat, and for the first time in ages, he smiled.

Rantz was considered the ringleader, and he was tried first. He faced three charges. First, he was charged with conspiring with others to resist the draft. Secondly, he was accused of being a member of the Knights of the Golden Circle. Lastly, he was charged with publicly expressing disloyal sentiments with the object of weakening the government's efforts to suppress the rebellion. Rantz was found guilty on all charges. He was sentenced to a fine of $1,000 and to serve two years' imprisonment at Fort Mifflin.

Jacob was unlucky enough to be the second prisoner tried. The day before his trial began, three men visited him in an isolated room. Colonel John Freeze introduced himself as lead defense counsel. He was assisted by Hamilton Aldricks and A. J. Herr. Colonel Freeze detested the overreaching power of the federal government. He saw the government as a tyrant, trampling the Constitution to bully any individual who spoke out against the war.

For the first time, Jacob heard the charges placed against him. Under section 25 of the 1863 Federal Draft Act, he stood accused of "entering into, confederating, and assisting in forming a combination to resist the execution of certain provisions of an Act of Congress, approved the third day of March 1863, entitled an act for enrolling and calling out the National forces, etc., and several supplements thereto." He was also charged with "the commission of an act of disloyalty against the Government of the United States, and uttering disloyal statements and opinions, with the object of defeating and weakening the power of the government in its efforts to suppress the unlawful rebellion now existing in the United States."

Also for the first time, his legal representatives learned their client was a pacifist and member of the Society of Friends. After much discussion, it was decided not to use his religion as a defense. It was feared that a military tribunal might consider Jacob a coward as well as disloyal. In addition, they were handicapped by not knowing who would appear as a witness against their client although they now had some inkling after the Rantz trial. In addition, they had been required to submit any questions in advance and in writing to the provost marshal.

It was decided that Jacob's defense would center around the lack of jurisdiction of the military tribunal, the questionable legality of the suspension of the writ of habeas corpus by the president, and the unconstitutionality of trial by other than a jury of his peers. Jacob preferred to have the case argued as one of freedom of religion. Jacob's parents had taught him that the freedoms of speech and religion were paramount. This is why they were included in the first rather than a later amendment. However, he was not learned in the law and bowed to the expertise of his lawyers.

Captain Francis Wessels, judge advocate, acted as the prosecutor. The military commission consisted of Colonel Charles Prevost, Major J. M. Fink, and Captain William Lee. Colonel Prevost was a large man standing about six feet tall. He was somewhat portly and had a receding red hairline. He hated his red hair, as it had caused much teasing and numerous fights when he was a child. To him, its only benefit was that it had attracted his wife, Leigh. She loved the color of his hair but admonished anyone speaking of her husband's red hair, noting that it was auburn. Prevost was ambivalent about his military career. He hated the desk job and paperwork. Yet, deep down, he was glad that he did not have a combat command. He constantly wondered how he would react under fire. It was not that he feared being killed so much as he was afraid of being crippled or suffering a long, agonizing death. As for the defendants appearing before him, he considered them to be fifth columnists and preferred to see them all convicted. Yet he had an underlying sense of fairness. As the trials would continue, he would become more convinced that the government's witnesses were unreliable and their case week. Unfortunately for Jacob, he was the second defendant to be tried, and the judge's revelation would not occur until much later.

On the day of his trial, Jacob was escorted to a makeshift courtroom. There were three members of the commission, his three attorneys, two prosecutors, and two other men. Jacob found one man vaguely familiar; the other was a total stranger. There were armed guards at every door. No other civilians were in the court. Large portraits of President Lincoln and Vice President Johnson appeared on the wall behind the military panel.

In his defense, Jacob would have an ally he did not know and would never meet. His name was Lambdin P. Milligan, and he hailed from Indiana. On October 5, 1864, Milligan was at home when he was arrested by forces acting on behalf of General Alvin P. Hovey, the military commander of the state of Indiana.

On October 21, Milligan was tried on charges similar to those brought against the Fishing Creek defendants. He was found guilty and was sentenced to hang. The sentence was approved by the president. With the consent of the United States district attorney for Indiana, the case was appealed to the Supreme Court. Basically, Milligan claimed that the president's repeal of the right of habeas corpus was illegal and that no military tribunal had a right to try him. One of Milligan's attorneys, J. J. Black, was originally from Pennsylvania, and he was in touch with Jacob's attorneys. At the time of Jacob's trial, Ex parte Milligan was fourteen months away from a decision by the Supreme Court.

Jacob pleaded not guilty to the charges. As a preliminary matter, Freeze raised three objections. First, the president had no legal right to revoke the right to habeas corpus, and therefore, the case should be heard in a federal district court. Secondly, the military commission had no right to try Jacob, as the federal civil courts were open and operating. Lastly, trial by a military court denied Jacob his right to a trial by a jury of his peers.

Colonel Freeze began, "May it please the court?" Under his breath he added, "Such as it is!" With regard to the issue of habeas corpus, it has been said that Congress granted that power to suspend said writ to the president by way of the Habeas Corpus Act of 1863. The Constitution gives Congress, and only Congress, the power to suspend said writ. We submit that a power granted by the Constitution may be conveyed only by constitutional amendment and not by a mere legislative act. Should it be otherwise, the provisions pertaining to the amendment of the Constitution are superfluous, as changes to the Constitution may be made by mere legislative fiat.

Freeze could have argued that the 1863 Act suspended rather than revoked the writ of habeas corpus. This would have meant that military authorities could arrest and hold civilians but could not try or punish them. However, this would mean the commission would have to uphold in part and strike down part of the law. Worse, it meant defendants could be held until the end of hostilities, when the writ would be revived. Then they would be tried by civilian authorities.

The other issues of trial in a civilian court and trial by jury are linked and were argued together. Freeze looked directly at Colonel Prevost. "For years—nay, for centuries—it has been the law in Great Britain that everyone accused of a crime has the right to a trial by jury. Such rule of law has been passed down to every nation ruled by British common law. It is the birthright of every American.

"The Magna Carta provides that 'no freeman shall be taken or imprisoned, or disseized or outlawed, or banished or in any way destroyed; nor will we pass upon him unless by lawful judgment of his peers, or the law of the land.'

"The petition of rights passed in the third year of the reign of Charles I provides 'that no man of what state or condition should be put out of his land or tenements, nor taken, nor imprisoned, nor disinherited, or put to death without due process of law.'

"In the common law case of *Grant v. Gould*, as reported in Hale Common Law C2, 36, 'martial law as of old does not exist in England at all and is contrary to the Constitution, and has been for a century totally exploded.' This is correct, both in war and peace.

"Our Constitution clearly states that 'the judicial power of the United States shall be vested in one Supreme Court, and in such inferior courts as Congress may from time to time ordain and establish.'"

Colonel Freeze paused and took a sip of water. "Any other exercise of judicial power tramples upon the Constitution, the sacred covenant that holds these states together. Rights to life, liberty, and property were put under the protection of the judiciary. The old alien and sedition acts are null and void. Yet government officials prosecute supposed political offenses as sedition, conspiracy, libel, and treason. It is to the credit of our Founding Fathers that such trials dare not be heard in open court. In closed court, information may be taken from sniveling spies who make merchandise of their oaths and trade in the blood of their fellow man."

Freeze looked to the judges for a clue as to the effectiveness of his argument. None was to be had. He continued, "Juries are not infallible, but they are the best protection for the innocent.

Montesquieu, DeTocqueville, Coke, and Blackstone have calmly judged and extolled the jury system. This is the reason for England's greatness and our most precious inheritance from the British Isles. No one can be free under a government that can punish without restraint. The Federalist noted the arbitrary power of convictions and punishment for pretended offenses had been the great engine of despotism in all ages and in all countries. Our forefathers were determined that not one drop of blood shed on the other side of the Atlantic in such fashion should sink into our grounds. A tyrannical government calls everybody a traitor who shows unwillingness to be a slave. The Constitution stands between the most patriotic citizen and statutes, which may place them at the basest minions that skulk about under the pay of the executive. It is the Constitution that lets one lie down in security and sleep the sleep of a free man. These rights remain in force and shall never be surrendered, and they shall be defended to the last extremity. The right to a trial by jury arose in the forests of Germany more than two thousand years ago and was carried to England by the Saxons. For a time, such right was extinguished by the Danes, but it was reestablished by Alfred the Great. It was trampled by the Normans but resurrected by the Great Charter. Edward II had the Earl of Lancaster executed after trial by a military court. Eight years later, the king and his lords in Parliament assembled, acknowledged with shame and sorrow that the execution was mere murder. Likewise, Queen Elizabeth, for reasons of state safety, ordered certain offenders tried by the military, but as haughty, imperious, and self-willed as she was, she was forced to yield. During an insurrection, the Lord Lieutenant of Ireland had Viscount Stormont tried as a traitor by the military, resulting in beheading. The lord lieutenant was impeached, Parliament was deaf, and the king himself could not bar Stafford's death as a traitor and murderer.

During upheaval, Charles I issued commissions for trial of his enemies by military laws, but he was obliged to concede his commissions were illegal.

"The world recognized our Constitution as the standard by which rights are to be measured, and every man who ever held office in this land has sworn to uphold it. The trial of all crimes shall be by jury, and all persons shall enjoy that privilege, and *no* person shall be held to answer in any other way. It is argued that the judgment under consideration was pronounced in a time of war, and it is therefore, at least, morally excusable. But it is precisely in the time of war and civil commotion that we should double the guards upon the Constitution. If health laws are to be relaxed, it ought certainly not be done at a time when pestilence is abroad. This judgment was not one of necessity. The commissioners have the choice to obey the law or disobey it. The government desired to remove these men out of this world, but there was no proof by which any court could take their liberty; therefore, it was necessary to create an illegal tribunal, which would convict them without proof. By such reasoning, it would be equally right to murder them. Nothing has led to more oppression than the pretense of state necessity.

"In 1815, General Jackson placed all civil authority in New Orleans under his command to save the city, and civil authority acquiesced. But after the city was saved, he stood before the court to be tried by law. The same judge who had declared Jackson's acts to be of necessity found his conduct illegal, and Jackson paid the penalty without a murmur.

"The Constitution may not be repealed in one state because there is war in another state. If the rights to life and liberty can be suspended, surely lesser rights of free speech, property, and search upon warrant can be obliterated without question. Thus, the president and Congress can make war a chronic condition and the slavery of the people perpetual. Ergo, a foreign potentate may shatter our Constitution without striking a single blow. Civil war can only be justified to uphold the constitutional rights of the people, not trample them down. Thus, when the Constitution is attacked from one side, its official guardian may assail it from the other. If the framers had intended the Constitution to apply only in the time of peace, they would have provided some other rule in the time of war. The rule should forever be *Salus populi suprema lex*—not *saul regis*. The safety of the people, not the safety of the ruler, is the supreme law.

"A military commission is not a court-martial, and it is not a civil court. It has no law of its own. The attorney general asserts the right of the executive, without judicial intervention, to capture, imprison, and kill any person to whom that government may choose to impute an offense. This is despotic and lawless. In effect, the attorney general argues that due to weighty reasons the state may set upon and kill Banquo. In uncivilized countries, the military is used to suppress. But in none of its forms can it be introduced into this court. We have no room for it. The ground here is all preoccupied by legal and free institutions. The right to kill and imprison citizens for political offenses may not be claimed in this country.

"This commission can deliver us from the body of this death. To that fearful extent, the destiny of this nation is in your hands.

"Our forefathers laid out many grievances against King George III in the Declaration of Independence. Some of those grievances are at issue here today. It would indeed be ironic if that tyrant's nation gives its people greater freedoms and protections than would our Constitution. The tyrant becomes the liberator and the liberator becomes—"

"Counselor Freeze," angrily interrupted Colonel Prevost. "We have heard enough hyperbole for one day. Save the rhetoric for another time. The issue is whether Jacob Saddler is guilty as charged or not." By this time Prevost was disturbed. It was not that he disagreed with many of the sentiments expressed by Freeze, but he was not about to listen to Freeze belittle the president as a tyrant.

Freeze was taken aback. Thus far, he had been given free reign. He continued with a lowered voice. "Your Honor, if I may conclude briefly. The Constitution lays out the procedures the executive must follow to arrest and convict any citizen. Only an amendment to that document can add or detract one wit from those procedures. The decision in this case may well have a profound impact on our nation. Should these draconian measures be upheld now, they may be applied at a future time, by a future government to God only knows what ends."

When the commission reconvened that afternoon, Jacob learned the identity of the two men he had seen that morning. Their names were Hugh Schultz and Richard Stiles. They were from the Benton area, and they were there to testify against Jacob.

Schultz took the stand, swore the oath, and testified he had heard Jacob Saddler speak out against the war at a Husbandry Association meeting. He alleged Jacob had said that the war was evil and unjust. Anyone participating in the war was unchristian and acting against the will of God. Shultz asserted Jacob further claimed that neither saving the Union nor freeing the slaves justify the massive loss of life, the injuries, or the hardships endured by the civilian population.

Stiles took the same oath and testified he had heard Jacob speak against the draft at the Bloomsburg market. He stated that Jacob said as the war was unjust, and so was the draft. He alleged Jacob had said that he would not submit to the draft and that no one else should submit either.

Jacob turned to Colonel Freeze and said he had made statements similar to those alleged by Schultz when he was asked about his Quaker beliefs. However, he denied stating that participation in the war was unchristian. He was aware that different religions interpreted the Good Book differently and that each individual's conscience might lead people in different directions. He asserted that he seldom attended the market at Bloomsburg and that he certainly did not make such statements there. Most of his opinions about the war and draft were made within the Society of Friends.

Cross-examinations of the men were similar. "To the best of your knowledge, is or was Jacob Saddler a Copperhead or a member of the group known at the Knights of the Golden Circle?"

"No, not that I know of."

"Is it your impression that Mr. Saddler was speaking on behalf of any political group or organization?"

"Can't say as I know what political group he might belong to."

"Do you have any proof or knowledge that the defendant in fact resisted the draft, counseled any drafted man not to report for duty, or engaged with anyone to counsel people to resist the draft?"

"No."

The commissioners conferred briefly and rendered their verdict. As to the charge that Jacob had formed any combination to resist the war or the draft, he was found not guilty. As to the charge that he had made disloyal statements that might weaken the war effort, he was found guilty. He was to be confined at Fort Mifflin for six months or, in lieu thereof, pay a fine of $500. Jacob was in a panic; he could not tolerate six months in a bombproof, and he did not have $500. Freeze assured him that the Philadelphia Society of Friends would pay $200 of the fine and that the local community around Benton would pay $100. Although it would take all his savings, Jacob could pay the remaining $200. He would be held briefly in Harrisburg until the fine was paid.

Of the remaining prisoners, six were found guilty of various charges of impeding the war effort. The sentences were Samuel Kline, two years; Benjamin Colley and Joseph Van Sickle, one year; John Lemons and Valentine Fell, six months; and William Appleman, one year or a $500 fine. Given the number of men apprehended, imprisoned and finally tried, it was not a sterling record.

And what, you may ask, happened in the case of *Ex parte Lambdin P. Milligan*? The court recognized the president's power to suspend the "privilege" of the writ of habeas corpus. However, the court removed the fangs from the law by explaining, as only a group of lawyers could, that "the suspension of the privilege of the writ of habeas corpus does not suspend the writ itself." In short, the suspension was temporary and to last only until the appropriate federal court had the opportunity to bring an indictment, if appropriate.

The court had numerous difficulties with the imposition of martial law and the trial of civilians in military courts in those areas, such as Indiana, that were not in rebellion and where the federal civilian courts were open and operating. Those difficulties included the constitutional provision "that the trial of all crimes, except in the case of impeachment, shall be by jury." The Fourth Amendment provided that a judicial warrant shall not be issued "without proof or probable cause supported by oath or affirmation." Then there is the Fifth Amendment that declares "that no person shall be held to answer for a capital or otherwise infamous crime unless on presentment by a grand jury, except in cases arising in the land or naval forces, or in the militia, when in actual service in the time of war or public danger, nor be deprived of life, liberty, or property without due process of law." Last, these were a violation of the Sixth Amendment guarantee of the right to trial by jury.

Although not part of the findings, the court noted that "during the late wicked rebellion, the temper of the times did not allow that calmness in deliberation and discussion so necessary to a correct conclusion of a purely judicial question. Now that the public safety is assured, this question, as well as others, can be discussed and decided without passion . . ."

Justice Davis, delivering the opinion of the court, wrote that "the Constitution of the United States is a law for rulers and people, equal, in war and peace and covers in the shield of its protection all classes of men, at all times and under all circumstances. No doctrine involving more pernicious consequences was ever invented by the wit of man than that any of its provisions can be suspended during any of the great exigencies of Government." Military commissions "can never be applied to citizens in States which have upheld the authority of the Government, and where, the courts are open and their process unobstructed. One of the plainest constitutional provisions was, therefore, infringed when Milligan was tried by a court not ordained and established by Congress.

"Another guarantee of freedom was broken when Milligan was denied a trial by jury . . . This right—one of the most valuable in a free country—is preserved to every one accused of a crime (except for military personnel). All other persons, citizens of states where the courts are open, if charged with a crime, are guaranteed the inestimable privilege of trial by jury. This privilege is a vital principle, underlying the whole administration of criminal justice; it is not held by sufferance, and cannot be frittered away on any plea of State or political necessity."

The court felt that if, in a time of war, the commander of an armed force has the power to suspend all civil rights, the "republican form of government is a failure, and there is an end of liberty regulated by law. Martial law, established on such a basis, destroys every guarantee of the Constitution and effectually renders the military independent of and superior to the civil power—the attempt to do which by the King of Great Britain was deemed by our fathers such an offense, that they assigned it to the world as one of the causes which impelled them to declare their independence."

There is an old adage that times of war make for poor law. Apparently, the court agreed. The opinion stated, "But it is insisted that the safety of the courts in time of war demand that their broad claim for martial law should be sustained. If this were true, it could be well said that a county preserved at the sacrifice of all cardinal principles of liberty is not worth the cost of preservation."

Chapter IX

ELECTIONS

The military raids of late August had been conducted with nary a hitch. One hundred desperados had been apprehended. Forty-five, deemed the greatest threat to public safety, had been locked in a bombproof in Fort Mifflin outside of Philadelphia. With the reduced threat to security, some of the occupying soldiers had been assigned similar duties in other counties. Others had been assigned duties more in line with the war effort.

Still, several hundred troops remained in northern Columbia County. The rationale provided by authorities was that deserters and drafted men were still at large. This was correct, but such persons could be found in many counties in the north. Few of those counties were blessed with the protection of so many soldiers.

Sporadic arrests continued to be made. As with the original arrests of August, most involved political dissidents rather than deserters or drafted men. As September turned to October, some began to think there was an ulterior motive for the presence of so many federal troops. Were they stationed there to influence the upcoming elections in October? Back then, statewide elections were held in October.

The primary target of the federal raids was Reverend A. R. Rutan. He was arrested in Luzerne County on August 31, 1864. Armed guards escorted him to Benton in Columbia

County, arriving at 10:00 p.m. The reverend was allowed to go where he wished until 1:00 p.m. the next day, when he was arrested again. General Cadwalader paroled him.

Reverend Rutan remained free until he was again arrested the night before the October elections. As he described it, "Six drunken soldiers hammered on my door and threatened to break it down unless I opened it. Immediately upon opening the door, I was arrested and handled very roughly. Due to confusion and their constant state of inebriation, it took us two days to arrive at Bloomsburg. As a result, I was forced to sleep on the ground for two nights. A day and a night were spent in Bloomsburg before I was transported to Harrisburg. There I appeared before Judge Advocate Wessels. He promised to release me if I would write down what I knew about secret meetings in the Benton area. Civility prevents me from relating my reply.

"While being held at Harrisburg, I was approached by a pale, thin man of about average height. He was probably in his midforties and had blond hair with a mustache and goatee. He introduced himself only as Mr. Pealer. He did not state under whose authority he acted but promised that I would be released and my family would not be bothered if I were to provide him with $65, a Devonshire heifer, and a fine dog. I did not know whether to take greater umbrage to the solicitation for a bribe or the scant value he placed upon my person. Political pressure was brought to bear, and I was released shortly after that encounter. It is common knowledge that certain members of Mr. Lincoln's administration will release prisoners for a price. I do not know if Mr. Pealer is one of them or if he could have obtained my release. I do know that if Mr. Pealer was enriched by such a sum, as well as a cow and a dog, that such ill-gotten gains did not come from me."

Less than a week later, Reverend Rutan was again arrested and taken to Harrisburg. Various unnamed military officers questioned him about alleged disloyalty. As they did not receive the answers they sought, the prisoner was transported to Philadelphia and incarcerated at Fort Mifflin. Political pressure was again brought to bear and President Lincoln finally pardoned him on March 1, 1865. He complained bitterly about his treatment and contended that his imprisonment had cost him at least $600 in lost crops. The alleged loss was offset in part by a contribution of $300 collected by his Democratic neighbors.

The day before the November 1864 elections, James McHenry of Luzerne County was arrested. He was detained until after Election Day. In 1866, he was elected to the state legislature.

David Lewis, a fifty-three-year-old farmer, was arrested at 11:00 p.m. the night before the elections. No charges were brought against him. He was released the following day after the polls had closed. Ezekiel Cole was likewise arrested and released.

Daniel Hartman, a crippled elections official for Benton Township, was arrested at the polls. No reason was ever given for his arrest. Thomas Downs of Bloom Township was also arrested at the polls and, like the others, released after the elections without being given any reason for his arrest.

Section 95 of Public Law 541, enacted on July 2, 1839, prohibited the presence of troops at polling places except for the purpose of voting. Despite this, eleven soldiers were present at the Centre Township polls. Ten to fifteen troops were present at the Beaver and Mount Pleasant polls. Ten to twelve soldiers were present at the Hemlock Township, and a like number made two arrests on Election Day at Fishing Creek Township.

Fifteen soldiers were present at Benton Township for state elections and about forty for the presidential election. At Briar Creek, one would-be voter was arrested; and in Jackson Township, eight to ten federals demanded the ballots. A similar occurrence was reported at Sugarloaf Township. During the presidential election, one officer, sword in hand, demanded that the election results be turned over to him. The poll watchers aligned themselves between the officer and ballot boxes. Risking their lives, they stood as one and refused the demand.

Just as the officer raised his sword, he had a moment of clarity, and his anger subsided. His orders were to maintain peace at the polls and to arrest any suspected felons who might attempt to vote. If any Democrats were dissuaded from voting by the mere presence of troops, well that would just be the cream on top of the milk. He did not have a free hand to initiate violence. How would it look if he were to kill or maim poll watchers? His superiors would not support him. Public opinion would be outraged. He would be left to fend for himself. What sin had the poll watchers committed? They were upholding their oaths to maintain the sanctity of the electoral process. If anything, they exceeded the call of duty by not stepping aside but by putting their lives on the line. The officer uttered a number of epithets under his breath as he sheathed his sword and left the polling place. His soldiers would remain outside. The pollsters would be left in peace to count the ballots.

Prior to the voting, Daniel Holter and William Heller of Hemlock Township were arrested. The soldiers took the two men and placed them in the custody of Sheriff Michael Furman. Furman considered the arrests to be illegal and protested vehemently. In the end, he had little choice but to accept the prisoners. Should he set them free, the federals would hold him responsible. To make matters worse, both men stated they wanted to vote. Sheriff Furman agreed.

Furman felt he was between the proverbial rock and a hard place. He was sure the men had been illegally detained and should be able to exercise their right to vote. On the other hand, they had been placed in his custody and in his jail. The sheriff sought out Senator Buckalew for advice and explained the situation to him.

"Hmmm," murmured the senator. He agreed with Furman as to the illegality of the arrests. "I see that does place you in quite a predicament. You say the troopers placed him in your custody, is that correct?"

Furman nodded.

"And both men have expressed their desire to vote?"

Furman nodded again.

"Let me think. Of course they can't vote from their jail cell. Both men would have to be present at the Hemlock Township polls. Suppose you were to personally escort them to the polls. They would still be in your custody. I believe that is all the officer required. He demanded they stay in your custody and be placed in your jail. But he did not require that they be in the jail at all times, just in your custody."

"Yes sir, that is about it," Furman replied.

The senator proposed that Sheriff Furman personally escort the men to the polls. That way, although free from jail temporarily, they would still be in his custody. It was agreed that if anything went wrong, Buckalew's name was not to be mentioned. In return, he would do what he could to help Furman.

The sheriff returned to the jail and related the plan to the two men, being careful not to mention Buckalew's name. Both Holter and Heller agreed to go along with it. It was decided that Furman would drive the men to the polls in his wife's carriage so that the men would be partially concealed. If they were to travel by horse or buckboard, the men would be conspicuous and raise suspicions among any Republicans who might have gotten wind of the arrests.

Early the next morning, Furman loaded the two men into the carriage. Both men had given their word that they would not try to escape. In those days, a man's word meant something. In return, the sheriff agreed they would not be handcuffed or restrained in any way.

Sheriff Furman was not fainthearted. He stood just over six feet tall and had a muscular blacksmith's build. He had dark hair and a thick mustache. His had piercing eyes, and his very presence diffused many tense situations. Those who were not intimidated by his appearance and chose to resist instantly regretted their choices. Furman remained undefeated in bars and back alleys.

Despite his reputation, Furman began imagining the presence of soldiers as he rounded every bend. Every oncoming rider was scanned for the presence of a blue tunic. None appeared. The sheriff stopped the buggy behind a grove of trees less than a hundred yards from the polling place. Both men approached the polls on foot. They were surprised to see troopers at the polls. Holter and Heller conferred briefly. They had come this far to vote, and vote they would. Both men acted in a normal fashion and were allowed to vote. The soldiers did not know the men had been arrested and let them pass.

True to their word, they returned to Sheriff Furman's custody. Having accomplished his mission, Furman was less apprehensive on the return trip. All went well until he turned the last bend before reaching the jail. To his dismay, he ran headlong into a squad of cavalry. The soldiers had been sent by Captain Dodge to take custody of the two prisoners. Upon hearing the sheriff had taken the men to vote, one trooper was dispatched to report to Provost Marshall Silver. The rest began what was to be a brief search.

At first, Furman could not believe his eyes. He had come this far only to be nabbed at the last minute. His mind rapidly began processing options. Should he run? A buggy against a squad of cavalry was not an option. Even if by a miracle he escaped, he would be hunted down. Should he have a shoot-out? For a moment, his palm rested on the handle of his pistol. His thumb was on the hammer. Outnumbered about ten to one, the odds were greatly against him. He did not know what he might be charged with, but it would be unwise to find out. The only sane option was to surrender. He placed his trust in Senator Buckalew's ability to unwind the mess. The confrontation was tense but peaceful. Holter and Heller were returned to jail and shortly thereafter released.

An armed guard escorted Sheriff Furman to Bloomsburg and then by train to Harrisburg. Furman assumed he would be sent to Fort Mifflin, as this had been the fate of others from that neck of the woods. Instead, he was held for several days and transferred to a penitentiary. The authorities were in a quandary on how to charge him. There was no law against entering a conspiracy to assist someone to vote.

True to his word, Furman did not mention that he had consulted with Senator Buckalew. The senator also was true to his word. Several of the original forty-five detainees had held minor positions in local government. None had the stature of a law enforcement officer. By this time, twenty-one of the original prisoners had been released. One, William Roberts, had died; and several others had been hospitalized, including John Yorks, R. Willis Davis, Ben Colley, John Rantz, and

Abraham Kline, who became ill, and George Hurliman, who was crippled by rheumatism. One had gone insane. Prospects for convicting all the remaining prisoners were not all that promising. Now they had a local sheriff detained in a state penitentiary without charge or conviction. Prisons were not safe places to house law enforcement officers. The citizens of Columbia County, most but not all Democrats, were on the warpath. Moreover, they had a United States senator leading the charge. Eventually, the military authorities threw up their hands and released Furman. As was the case with the prior detainees, he returned home a hero.

Prior to the October elections, the Republicans were certain they would lose several Northern states in the November presidential election. Kentucky was beyond the pale. One of the potential problems was Pennsylvania. After the October elections, they were reasonably confident that Lincoln would carry the Commonwealth.

Did the arrests and the presence of troops at the poll affect voter turnout? A quick look at election statistics indicates that such threats had a profound impact when judged against voter turnout in state elections the previous year.

Township	1863	1864
Fishing Creek	300	192
Benton	209	112
Sugarloaf	166	106

Throughout the remainder of the state, voter participation rose between 1860 and 1864.

Another anomaly arose in the presidential election of November 1864. Although the Commonwealth and nation voted for Lincoln, Columbia County held steadfast for General George McClellan.

	McClellan	Lincoln
County	3,367	1,914
State	277,443	296,292
Nation	1,803,787	2,206,938

Columbia was one of several counties in the state that voted for McClellan in 1864. Included in those counties were nearby Northumberland and Schuykill counties. Lincoln's 3.5 percent victory margin in Pennsylvania was the third lowest for the Republican in 1864. Still, it was better than losing in Delaware and New Jersey and losing badly in Kentucky.

At its height, the occupation of Columbia County called for the presence of one thousand troops led by a general. After the election of 1864, Captain Dodge led the remaining soldiers. They departed between November 13 and December 1. Captain Dodge left to "clear out" Philipsburg in Clearfield County.

Democrats would continue to refer to the events of August to December 1864 as the Invasion of Columbia County or the Occupation of Columbia County. The Republicans referred to it by its better-known name, the Fishing Creek Confederacy. Whatever the name, it would be the Democrats who would have the last say on the issue, at least at that time.

Chapter X

THE NOB HILL MEETING

After the assassination of Lincoln and the inauguration of Andrew Johnson, the Democratic leaders of Columbia County called for a meeting of all party members at Nob Hill at Megargell's Grove. On Tuesday, August 29, 1865, the Democrats convened to "pass resolutions concerning the outrages perpetrated against certain citizens of the county, to refute irresponsible claims by Republicans, to record the true events arising out of the invasion of the county by Union troops, and to protest various dangerous trends displayed by the government in Washington."

The Republicans dubbed the meeting a case of "the bugs finally emerging from the woodwork to show their true colors, after other members of the same clan had assassinated President Lincoln, thereby succeeding in enabling that incompetent Johnson to take office and obstruct all advances towards the justice and unity our boys have died for."

Senator Buckalew organized the meeting with the aid of Colonel Freeze. A one-hundred-foot-long speakers' platform was built. It was festooned with garlands, flags, and lamps. Horses and carriages lined the roadway into the grove. Booths and roving vendors provided food, drinks, and souvenirs. Seventeen musicians from Danville attended to help set the tone. Eight meetings and thirteen speakers were scheduled for the three-day event.

Reverend J. W. Lescher of Bloomsburg gave the opening prayer giving thanks for the return of peace. He was followed by Reverend Rutan who spoke on the political persecution caused by the Columbia County Invasion. Charles Barkley, a local attorney, read from Jefferson's first inaugural address. He extolled the virtues of individual freedom, habeas corpus, and trial by jury so scorned by Republicans.

Colonel Freeze stated that he opposed the secession of the South. He was equally opposed to and would have no association with that Northern party that violated the sacred trust of the American people and pronounced the Constitution to be "a covenant with death and an agreement with hell." He held that had the Democratic Party prevailed, the Union would have been saved without the slaughter, debt, and disgrace of subverting the privilege of white citizens to vote. The colonel roared that the state ordinances of secession were null and void. Therefore, it was the Northern faction that pronounced the Union legally dissolved and malignantly labored to prevent its restoration. He argued that the general government sought to force Negro suffrage upon the states against the will of the people and contrary to existing law. That was a high crime against the Constitution. Pounding his fist on the dais, he shouted that there was a movement afoot to Africanize a large portion of the country, to degrade the white race morally, socially, and politically to the low level of the black. He called for a prohibition of murder by military commissions and reduction of the enormous national debt by reduction of army and naval forces. The colonel argued that saying those who fought to preserve the Union actually fought to free the Negro was a gross insult to their patriotism.

Wesley Wirt, another local attorney, lectured that the Constitution didn't interfere with domestic institutions including slavery. Lincoln said he raised the army to save the

Union when his real purpose was to free the slaves. Accordingly, the army was raised under false pretenses, and abolitionists were snakes in the grass.

Colonel Victor Piollet of Bradford County kicked off the evening session. He stated some veterans felt the Democrats did not support them because of false newspaper reports. The colonel argued that veterans were better men than the stay-at-home Republicans who avoided service. He proposed that "loyal Republicans had burdened the government with hundreds of millions of debt while ridiculing those who worried about such debt. All the time loyal Republicans filled their pockets with greenbacks from war profiteering." Piollet felt that many people had enriched themselves by purchasing war bonds and not paying taxes. He worried Republican policies would establish an "aristocracy of wealth." Lastly, he invited all Republicans who opposed equality of the Negroes to join the Democratic Party.

Senator Buckalew was the last speaker of the day. It was his view that all Southern states remain in the Union. He urged all Republicans who felt otherwise to immediately move to readmit them without any preconditions such as Negro suffrage. Republicans were accused of supporting the Negro vote only to increase the number of Republicans. He argued that the Republican Party was a Northern party and that George Washington had been right to warn that parties formed on a sectional basis would be fatal to peace and prosperity. He felt that just as Pennsylvania had abolished slavery, Southern states should have been allowed to do the same over time. After all, the South had not interfered with the Commonwealth's domestic policy of abolishing slavery. In conclusion, he stated that "the Emancipation Proclamation will always be remembered as a mere legal trick, and the war was neither the fault of the North nor the South but of Lincoln's party."

The first resolution passed by the meeting confirmed their faith in the Union and rejected secession as a solution to federal problems. The resolution was hailed by the Republican press as the "first, last, and only sane, logical and nontreasonable statement to come from the entire meeting."

The second resolution was not so pleasing to the ruling party. It decried the use of government power to force Negro suffrage on the states against the will of the people. The resolution ended by supporting President Johnson's attempt to save the land from "the curse of Negro equality."

Day two of the meeting opened with thirty of the Fort Mifflin prisoners taking the stage to thunderous applause. Senator Buckalew again spoke. "And what of those who would have us accept equality for the Negro? Will they permit a big black buck to sit at their dinner table? No, sir, they will not, but they will expect you to let him marry your daughter."

Colonel Freeze followed by retelling the story of the Columbia County Invasion in satirical terms. He ended his story by stating, "It's too bad that the fort with cannons, smuggled no doubt through the Union lines, that those brave soldiers marched so far to capture what turned out to be a huckleberry picnic."

Mr. Freeze then turned serious, noting the invasion was made possible by suspension of the writ of habeas corpus, thus allowing the military to hold civilians on false and frivolous charges and subordinate civilian power to the military. Rumors of The Army of Fishing Creek, made up of drafted men, were false. There was no evidence that the unknown parties who shot Lieutenant Robinson were drafted men or that they had fired first. The only crime committed by the citizens of northern Columbia County was to vote Democratic. True, there were drafted men in the county but in a lower percentage of many counties in the North. None of the hundred men rounded up proved to be a drafted man or deserter. Their arrests were without due process and in violation of the Constitution. The supposed rebels were all arrested peaceably in their homes. They were neither armed nor organized. No cannons or rifle pits were found. The whole fiasco was the fault of the lying abolitionist press of Bloomsburg. He characterized the troops as capturing crowing cocks and slaughtering grunting pigs. Freeze noted General Cadwalader had pronounced the whole affair a farce but lacked the manliness to rectify the situation. Many citizens allegedly provided the occupying forces with cakes, pies, and good whiskey. In return, the same troops tore down fences, cut down trees, dug up potatoes, stripped cornfields, and killed sheep and chickens while refusing to pay for such damage.

The colonel berated soldiers armed with rifles and bayonets at the polls. He alleged locals were locked up with niggers and bounty jumpers in conditions more filthy than pigpens. In doing so, the Republicans had cost the taxpayers a half million dollars and trampled on the Constitution as if it were an old piece of parchment.

Wednesday afternoon began with Senator Buckalew ascending the platform to deride Lincoln on another matter. "Do you know why Lincoln removed General McClellan from his rightful place as head of the Union army? I am sure no one here believed those lies spread by Stanton that it was because he failed to push the fight, for I assure you that to do so at the time would have resulted in a slaughter of our boys. No, sir! General McClellan is an honorable man, not a coward. He was removed for political reasons and political reasons alone. Old Abe knew that if McClellan remained at the head of the Union forces and ran for president as a Peace Democrat, that McClellan, not Lincoln, would soon be president. Lincoln and Stanton placed him in a position where he would be defeated and relieved of his command if he attacked and relieved for failure to press the enemy if he did not attack. Even after this, Old Abe was not so sure of himself, so he decided to let the soldiers in the field vote! Stanton then had the officers order all soldiers to vote for Lincoln. Not only that, but Negro soldiers were ordered to vote two or three times, and Republican officers refused to count Democratic votes. This is the danger of letting soldiers vote."

Freeze then entered into public evidence a letter from Senator Buckalew dated December 26, 1858. At the time, Buckalew was a representative to Quito and urged resistance to Negro equality. In the letter, it was explained that Ecuador was so far behind the United States because "the Spaniards have intermixed with inferior races and have become sluggish and backwards."

The afternoon session opened with a poem titled "This Old Hat."

When this old hat was made,
King George was on the throne;
Our fathers all were rebels then
And fought for Washington.
The Tories cheered for ol' King George
The Revolution through
And bragged about their loyalty,
Ere this old hat was new.

When this old hat was new,
There was no public debt:
No Greenbacks took the place of Gold,
No Millionaire had yet

His pile of dirty lucre spent,
On which no tax was due;
But each man fairly paid his tax,
When this old hat was new.

When this old hat was new,
Elections were still free,
And everyman was thought to have,
A right to liberty;
Arrests were made by course of law,
Trials were speedy too;
And Seward rang no little bell,
When this old hat was new.

When this old hat was new,
This land was in its prime;
Miscegenation was untaught
In all this happy clime;
And white folks then were thought as good
As Sambo, Nappy or Sue;
But things have sadly changed about
Since this old hat was new.

Colonel Wellington Ent—yes, another attorney—addressed the soldiers in the crowd. "We left together in 1860, fought together, and now returned together all for the perpetuity of the Union. You were treated as returning heroes, but now, if you do not endorse all acts of the administration, you are called a traitor."

Ent picked up where Freeze left off by calling McClellan the hero of the Peninsular Campaign, Antietam, and South Mountain. "The general was hounded by the northern press for not pursuing the enemy after Antietam, when his army was ill supplied and many men lacked shoes. He forced the enemy back to Warrenton. For this, he was removed from his position by politicians from New England. Afterward, the Union suffered bitter defeats under his two successors."

Captain Charles Brockway followed by stating that the Northern states should not have fought against secession, as many states, especially New England, had once advocated such a doctrine. In his first inaugural address, Lincoln admitted he had neither the inclination nor right to interfere with slavery. "The war was started to save the Union but was prostituted to free the slaves. (The word "prostituted" brought gasps from the ladies and chuckles from most of the men.) When fought to save the Union, the government had more volunteers than it could accept. When fought to free the slaves, it was necessary to draft men and to use Negro troops." He blamed the deaths of 1,700 soldiers at Andersonville on the government's insistence of including Negroes in prisoner exchanges, a demand resisted by the South.

Brockway then turned to the Declaration of Independence to point out the Founding Fathers' objection to George III's rule. "He has erected a multitude of new offices and sent hither swarms of officers to harass our people and eat out our subsistence. He has effected to render the military independent of, and superior to, the civil power . . . For depriving us, in many cases, the benefit of a trial by jury." He went on to allege that as an officer, he had seen how the voting was rigged. Brockway further claimed that Negro soldiers were kept safely in reserve. When forced to fight, they fled, as at Petersburg. He too felt the colonies of Spain fell because the Spanish had not the self-respect to remain uncontaminated by inferior races. Hence, the people south of the United States are not energetic, virtuous, or prosperous.

The Honorable John Cresswell ended the afternoon session with his poem, "Our Cause in Truth."

> Pure as the virgin stripes which wave
> O'er freedoms everlasting youth,
> And spotless as the soldier's grave,
> Then let our motto be;
> Our country, cause and liberty—
> Our nation and nation's love
> The rights of white men, Freedom's cause!"

The meeting that evening was opened with the singing of "A Darkey Ditty." The words were printed on leaflets and distributed to the crowd. The usual singing by catbirds and crickets in that tranquil area of rural Pennsylvania was now drowned out by the sound of untrained voices straining to make the words fit the melody and thereby present some semblance of a song.

> The Union they pretend to save,
> Which they had cursed before;
> And Wilson, Sumner, Wade and Chase,
> Went in for bloody war;
> Oh! Let them but the darkey free,
> They would ask no more;

> The war went on, the contraband
> Soon got the inside track,
> And Wilson, Sumner, Chase and Wade,
> All jumped upon his back;
> Oh! Let them but the darkey have,
> They would not ask any more;

They rode him fiercely through the fight,
And yelled with might and main,
And all their torchlight followers got
The darkey on the brain;
Oh! If they could the nigger free,
They would ask no more;

But now the darkeys all are free,
The master they ignore;
Yet Phillips, Sumner, Chase and Wade
Now howl for something more;
But Phillips, Sumner, Chase and Wade
Now howl for something more;

The Yankee hosts of Greenback Chase,
We see from day to day;
A raking among the darkey crowd,
Way down on Charleston Bay;
Oh! Give us now the darkey votes
And we won't ask any more;

But when the darkey gets the vote,
An equal he will be;
And Phillips, Sumner, Chase and Wade
Will ask his wench to tea,
And Phillips, Sumner, Chase and Wade
Will ask his wench to tea;

> Then comes the last grand finale,
> There is but one step more,
> Miscegenation is the word,
> By which they seek for power;
> Oh! Give them but the darkey wench,
> And they will ask no more.

Following the song, Mr. Fraugh, who was educated at Kingston Seminary, delivered a speech condemning the cowardice of Negro troops, stating they had not done enough to warrant the right to vote. "And although those Nigger boys broke and fled with the first shots, they were rounded up and marched ahead of the white soldiers whenever we had a parade! If the Negroes are to vote because they fought, what of the white soldiers age eighteen to twenty, and what of immigrants in the Irish Brigade? Why not the Indians? What next?

"Republicans claim an act of Congress gave the president the power to suspend the right of habeas corpus. Such right belongs solely to Congress and *delegatus non potest delegari* (the agent cannot delegate another in his stead). If this is allowed, then Congress may delegate all of its powers to the executive and create despotism."

On the last day, the Honorable Heister Clyman of Berks County, a Pennsylvania senator, contended that Republicans wanted all former rebels' property above $10,000 to be forfeited. He prayed that the black vote would never be inalienable. Senator Clyman held Massachusetts in particular scorn, as she alone had begged, bought, and hired black men to fill her ranks. He argued that those who executed civilians under the supposed authority of military tribunals were as guilty of murder as Cain.

E. R. Keeler, Esquire, claimed the abolitionists had declared the Democratic Party dead. "If so, you stand before me as the liveliest-looking corpses I ever beheld." He later noted, "We have the mastiff and the bloodhound, and it is impossible to make one do the work of the other. It may be possible to degrade the white man to the level of the Negro, but I say it is utterly impossible to elevate the Negro to the standard of the white man."

One of the last speakers compared the Republicans and the Constitution to a woodsman and a tree.

> Woodsman spare that tree!
> Touch not a single bough!
> In youth, it sheltered me,
> And I'll protect it now.
> 'Twas my forefathers hand
> That placed it near its cot;
> There woodsman let it stand;
> Thy axe shall harm it not.
>
> That old familiar tree,
> Whose glory and renown
> Are spread o'er land and sea—
> And wouldst thou hew it down?
> Woodsman forebear thy stroke!
> Cut not its earth-bound ties;
> Oh, spare that aged oak,
> Now towering to the skies.
> My mother kissed me here;
> My father pressed my hand—
> Forgive this foolish tear,

But let that old oak stand.
Old tree! The storm still brave!
And woodsman leave the spot;
While I've a land to save,
Thy axe shall harm it not.

Senator Buckalew summarized the sins of Lincoln and the Republicans. The audience went home with joy in their hearts, each to hate his fellow man in his own fashion. Except for the desire to save the Union, it truly was a meeting that would have brought a smile to Nathan Bedford Forrest.

SENATOR CHARLES ROLLIN BUCKALEW

was born on December 28, 1821, in Fishing Creek Township. He read law in Berwick and was admitted to the bar in 1843. In 1845, he was appointed prosecuting attorney of Columbia County, and in 1854, he was appointed commissioner to Paraguay.

Buckalew returned to Pennsylvania. In 1856, he was elected to the state senate. He became chairman of the State Democratic Committee in 1857. During that year, he helped revise the state penal code.

From 1858 to 1861, he was back in South America as minister resident of Ecuador. He returned home and was elected to the United States Senate by his peers in the state legislature. He ran on a plank to oppose repeal of the Fugitive Slave Act. Buckalew was reelected to the U.S. Senate in 1869. The senator was a delegate to the State Constitutional Convention in 1873. After his term in the Senate, he was elected to the House of Representatives in 1876 and reelected in 1880.

Throughout his public career, Buckalew was known as a logical but boring speaker. He was considered to be honest and straightforward. Thus, he often drew support from the Republican opposition. He was a champion of proportional representation, arguing that each state elector should have the number of votes equal to the number of the state's representatives in the House. The senator believed each elector could divide (or not) such votes as they saw fit.

Buckalew was always a man tied to his land, and his hobby was botany. He passed away on May 19, 1899, and was mourned as one of the greatest men to have arisen in the county.

GENERAL GEORGE CADWALADER

was born in Philadelphia on May 16, 1806. He was an attorney and served as a brigadier general under Winfield Scott in the Mexican-American War. After the Battle of Chapultepec, he was promoted to major general. In 1844, he helped quell riots by the Know Nothings.

Governor Andrew Curtain appointed Cadwalader head of the Pennsylvania Volunteers in 1861. The first encampment of troops during the Civil War was at Camp Cadwalader at Locust Point, Maryland, near Fort McHenry. During this time, he ordered the arrest of John Merryman, a Maryland civilian, for recruiting forces for the Confederacy. The chief justice of the Supreme Court, John Taney, issued a writ of habeas corpus for Merryman. Cadwalader ignored the writ, noting that President Lincoln had suspended the writ of habeas corpus. In response, Taney issued a contempt citation. Guards at Fort McHenry denied the U.S. marshal entry and the writ was never served.

The above led to the Supreme Court case of *Ex parte .Merryman*, in which the court ruled the president had no right to suspend the writ of habeas corpus, as the Constitution clearly gave such power only to Congress. The court noted that under the common law, even English monarchs could not suspend that writ. It also noted an 1807 opinion by Chief Justice John Marshall concluding such actions violated the Fourth and Fifth Amendments.

Cadwalader was appointed commander of the First Division of the Army of the Shenandoah and fought in multiple campaigns. Having defied the Supreme Court, he was not one to yield to political pressure when later acting as commander of the District of the Susquehanna in the Fishing Creek affair.

In April 1865, Cadwalader was chief commander of the ceremonies following the death of Lincoln. He founded the Military Order of the Loyal Legion of the United States, a veteran's organization. The general died on February 3, 1879.

COLONEL JOHN FREEZE

was born on November 4, 1825, in Lycoming County, Pennsylvania. He attended the Danville Academy and read law in that town. Freeze was admitted to the bar in 1848. From 1863 to 1869, he acted as the registrar and recorder for Columbia County.

In 1872, he was chosen as a member of the state Constitutional Convention. However, he relinquished his position in favor of Senator Buckalew. Freeze edited Buckalew's book, *Proportional Representation*. In 1883 he penned the *History of Columbia County Pennsylvania*. The work stands as an excellent source on the Fishing Creek Confederacy.

If Colonel Freeze dedicated his life to anything, it was to the cause of the underdog. Therefore, he took the case of those arrested in the Fishing Creek Confederacy. The highlight of his career was the defense of three Mollie Maguires: Patrick Hester, Peter McHugh, and Patrick Tully. The Mollies were a group of Irish miners who struck back at mine owners and operators for the horrid conditions they experienced in the anthracite coal industry in northeastern Pennsylvania.

The proverbial writing on the wall in those cases came during jury selection. Over Freeze's objection, the judge seated two jurors who, although stating they believed the defendants to be guilty, promised they would not allow such preconceptions to affect their decision. No jurors were of Irish Catholic descent or from coal towns. Freeze argued that the prosecution blamed the Mollies and the Ancient Order of Hibernians "with every crime that was committed, whether it be by an Englishman, an Irishman, or a Welshman." He also argued unsuccessfully that at the time of the alleged murders, the Mollie Maguires didn't exist. The chief prosecution witness, Manus Tull, was pardoned of his own crimes under questionable circumstances.

Appeals were denied on questionable legal grounds, and all three defendants were eventually executed. The short-drop hangings were too short, and the men thrashed around for several minutes before dying.

Years later, Freeze's death was considered a great loss to the local bar and the community as a whole.

MICHAEL P. KELLY

began his military career when he enlisted in the Irish Brigade. What else would an Irish lad from New York City in search of employment and adventure do? Due to his literacy and knowledge of the Irish language, he was placed on the staff of General Thomas Francis Meagher, the founder of the Irish Brigade. He became a favorite of Meagher's and was soon promoted to captain. Kelly fought bravely in his first action but took a Minie-ball in his left hip. The surgeon removed bone chips but could not repair the nerve damage. As a result, Kelly could neither lead infantry nor ride without extreme pain. Strings were pulled, and he landed at Fort Mifflin, where he could both serve and recuperate. He often cursed his injury. However, considering the casualty rate the brigade suffered in numerous battles, his injury and reassignment surely saved his life.

Kelly, like many in the brigade, joined the Fenian cause. The Fenians hatched a plan to invade Canada and hold captured provinces in exchange for the repeal of the Act of Union and Ireland's freedom. Michael was promoted to the rank of major in the Fenian Army. In June 1866, he led a force of 250 men on a raid of Niagara. The total force of 1,000-1,300 men under the command of Colonel John O'Neill routed Canadian militia at the battles of Ridgeway and Fort Eire.

Upon hearing of the invasion, the authorities in Washington became alarmed and ordered the arrest of the Fenians in the area. They also had naval gun boats cut off all supplies and reinforcements. Support from local Irish-Canadians and French never materialized. The Fenians retreated in the face of British regulars and surrendered to American authorities.

Kelly's mentor, Meagher, had been appointed Secretary of the Territory of Montana. He arranged for Kelly's release to join him there. Kelly never arrived in Montana. Rumors alleged he was killed by Indians or died of natural causes in the wilderness. Meagher disappeared after falling off a riverboat under mysterious circumstances. No trace of either man was ever found.

JACOB SADDLER

returned to his farm a broken young man. He had been mortified by his arrest, confinement, and trial. His fate had been beyond his control, and he felt helpless—less than a man.

As to the death of Corporal Brown, he was ambivalent. On one hand, he felt great remorse at having taken the life of another person. Yet the act had eased his burden and led to the realization that violence could be a viable option. Even that realization made him feel badly. It was as if he had betrayed his parents' teachings and, in the process, his parents.

Upon release from prison, he found himself with money to spend and time to kill. It was a bad combination. For the first time, he entered a saloon. His first shot of whiskey made him gag. Jacob noticed the smirks from the other patrons, the same looks he had so often received from the prison guards. He would drink enough to prove he was as good as they were.

On the train ride home, Jacob noticed a feeling of contentment and security. The feelings of helplessness and anger vanished. His problems seemed almost comical. He was to continue drinking. Drinking at taverns led to confrontations. He learned it was better to buy a bottle, return home, sit on the porch, prop up his legs, and drink in solitude.

After months of drinking, Jacob experienced stomach pain. The solution was to self-medicate. His pain would always go away, but it always came back stronger. One night, he noticed his stomach was rigid. He self-medicated and fell asleep, never to awaken. Jacob died the victim of a massive ulcer.

The young man was laid to rest in the family plot. Katherine was one of the few people to attend the burial. Beside Jacob was a small grave containing the remains of his best friend, his loyal dog Toby.

KATHERINE WINDER

was to become a lifelong pacifist, but she could not bring herself to join the Society of Friends. She took up nursing and helped numerous Civil War veterans. By the end of the war, the seemingly endless suffering had taken its toll. Katherine sought a new career and decided on teaching. She entered the Bloomsburg Literary Institute and was one of the first women to graduate from the newly named Bloomsburg Normal School.

Katherine found that she missed nursing and joined the American Red Cross. The highlight of her career came in her mid-forties, when she acted as one of Clara Barton's assistants after the Johnstown flood. She arrived on the scene while Ms. Barton was still at the nation's capital. Katherine proved especially adept at raising money. She often reminded potential donors of her favorite verse from Isaiah—"if you pour yourself out for the hungry and satisfy the desire of the afflicted, then shall your light rise in the dark and your gloom be as midday." Despite her kind heart, she could never bring herself to forgive Andrew Carnegie, Henry Clay Frick, and Andrew Mellon as well as other members of the South Fork Fishing and Hunting Club. These millionaires could have prevented the disaster by spending a small amount of their vast fortunes to repair the South Fork dam before it burst, sending its deadly cargo rushing to Johnstown.

Katherine aided the wounded during the Spanish-American War. She was thankful the war was brief and the casualties minimal compared to the previous war.

Nurse Winder came out of retirement to assist during World War I. She was appalled at the new and marvelous devices invented to make killing one's fellow beings more efficient. Once, a warrior's life depended on his skill. Now one could be killed from hundreds of yards away by machine guns that could fire faster than a whole company of men. There were artillery shells that could inflict massive casualties from miles away and cause the constant shaking of the shell-shocked. Then there was the gas; gas that blinded soldiers and ate out their lungs.

Katherine passed away a few years later. Numerous dignitaries attended her funeral. There were a handful of Civil War veterans and a contingent from Johnstown. However, her final thoughts had not been of all those she had aided over the years, but of a young man named Jacob and things that might have been.

Appendix

COMPARATIVE PRESIDENTIAL VOTING RECORD OF COLUMBIA COUNTY, STATE, AND NATION 1860-2008

1860

	Breckenridge	Douglas	Lincoln	Bell
County	2,367	86	1,873	14
State	16,765	178,871	268,036	2,770
Nation	848,256	1,382,713	1,865,593	592,906

1864

	McClellan	Lincoln
County	3,367	1,914
State	277,443	296,292
Nation	1,803,787	2,206,938

1868

	Seymour	Grant
County	4,002	2,143
State	277,443	342,280
Nation	1,803,787	3,013,421

1872

	Greeley	Grant
County	3,001	2,009
State	213,027	349,249
Nation	2,843,446	3,596,745

1876

	Tilden	Hayes
County	4,394	2,069
State	361,570	385,212
Nation	4,284,020	4,036,576

1880

	Hancock	Garfield	Weaver
County	4,598	2,236	192
State	407,428	444,704	22,656
Nation	4,414,082	4,453,295	345,947

1884

	Cleveland	Blaine	Other
County	4,338	2,443	275
State	394,772	472,827	32,204
Nation	4,918,507	4,850,293	282,892

1888

	Cleveland	Harrison	Other
County	4,676	2,484	281
State	446,633	526,151	24,844
Nation	5,537,857	5,447,129	398,291

1892

	Cleveland	Harrison	Watson	Other
County	4,929	2,336	356	24
State	451,904	516,011	26,021	8,714
Nation	5,555,426	5,182,690	292,833	1,029,846

1896

	Bryan	McKinley	Other
County	4,888	3,280	516
State	427,125	728,300	38,930
Nation	6,379,830	7,098,474	421,553

1900

	Bryan	McKinley	Other
County	4,982	2,954	454
State	424,232	712,665	36,313
Nation	6,356,734	7,218,491	389,342

1904

	Parker	Roosevelt	Other
County	4,196	3,635	415
State	337,998	840,949	57,791
Nation	5,084,233	7,628,464	805,486

1908

	Bryan	Taft	Other
County	5,373	3,718	402
State	446,728	745,779	72,899
Nation	6,412,294	7,675,320	796,651

1912

	Wilson	Taft	Roosevelt
County	4,905	889	3,086
State	395,697	273,360	548,589
Nation	6,296,547	3,486,720	5,251,227

1916

	Wilson	Hughes	Other
County	5,785	3,013	389
State	521,784	703,823	71,685
Nation	9,127,695	8,533,507	866,661

1920

	Cox	Harding	Other
County	6,965	6,238	462
State	503,843	1,218,216	130,559
Nation	9,133,092	16,153,115	1,482,406

1924

	Davis	Coolidge	LaFollette
County	7,390	7,336	743
State	409,192	1,401,481	307,567
Nation	8,386,242	15,723,789	4,831,706

1928

	Smith	Hoover	Thomas
County	5,304	14,362	115
State	1,067,586	2,055,382	18,647
Nation	15,015,464	21,427,123	267,478

1932

	Roosevelt	Hoover	Thomas
County	10,498	8,363	
State	1,295,948	1,453,546	91,223
Nation	22,821,277	15,761,254	884,885

1936

	Roosevelt	Landon	Lemke
County	14,196	9,745	
State	2,353,987	1,690,200	67,468
Nation	27,752,648	16,681,862	892,378

1940

	Roosevelt	Wilkie	Other
County	12,521	9,544	
State	2,171,035	1,889,848	17,831
Nation	27,313,945	22,347,744	240,424

1944

	Roosevelt	Dewey	Other
County	5,143	5,315	
State	1,940,479	1,835,054	19,260
Nation	25,612,916	22,017,929	346,218

1948

	Truman	Dewey	Wallace	Thomas
County	9,357	9,428		
State	1,752,426	1,902,197	55,161	11,351
Nation	24,179,347	21,991,292	1,157,328	139,569

1952

	Stevenson	Eisenhower	Other
County	8,179	11,373	
State	2,146,269	2,415,789	18,911
Nation	27,375,090	34,075,529	301,323

1956

	Stevenson	Eisenhower	Other
County	8,978	13,272	
State	1,981,769	2,585,252	9,482
Nation	26,028,028	35,579,180	414,120

1960

	Kennedy	Nixon	Other
County	9,322	15,310	19
State	2,556,282	2,439,956	10,303
Nation	34,220,984	34,108,157	503,341

1964

	Johnson	Goldwater	Other
County	13,885	8,982	36
State	3,130,954	1,673,657	18,079
Nation	43,127,041	27,175,754	336,489

1968

	Humphrey	Nixon	Wallace
County	8,187	12,202	1,797
State	2,259,403	2,090,017	378,582
Nation	31,271,839	31,783,783	9,901,118

1972

	McGovern	Nixon	Other
County	7,222	14,187	900
State	1,796,951	2,714,521	80,633
Nation	29,173,222	47,168,710	1,402,095

1976

	Carter	Ford	McCarthy
County	12,051	11,508	366
State	2,328,677	2,205,604	50,584
Nation	40,831,881	39,148,634	740,460

1980

	Carter	Reagan	Anderson
County	9,449	12,426	1,197
State	1,937,540	2,261,872	292,921
Nation	35,480,115	43,903,230	5,719,850

1984

	Mondale	Reagan	Other
County	8,254	14,402	62
State	2,228,131	2,584,323	32,449
Nation	37,577,352	54,455,472	620,409

1988

	Dukakis	Bush	Other
County	7,767	12,114	140
State	2,194,944	2,300,087	41,220
Nation	41,809,476	48,886,597	898,613

1992

	Clinton	Bush	Perot
County	8,261	9,742	5,683
State	2,239,164	1,791,841	902,667
Nation	44,909,806	39,104,550	19,743,821

1996

	Clinton	Dole	Perot
County	8,379	8,234	3,654
State	2,215,819	1,801,169	430,984
Nation	47,400,125	39,198,755	8,085,402

2000

	Gore	Bush	Nader
County	8,975	12,095	663
State	2,485,967	2,281,127	103,392
Nation	51,003,926	50,460,110	2,883,105

2004

	Kerry	Bush	Other
County	10,679	16,052	138
State	2,938,095	2,793,847	37,648
Nation	59,028,439	62,040,610	1,224,499

2008

	Obama	McCain	Nader
County	13,230	14,477	264
State	3,276,363	2,655,885	42,977
Nation	69,499,428	59,950,323	739,278

BIBLIOGRAPHY

Barton, Edwin. *Columbia County History*. Bloomsburg, Pennsylvania, 1984.

Battle, John. *History of Columbia and Montour Counties, Pennsylvania*. Chicago: A. Warner and Company, 1887.

Burman, W. Dean. *Presidential Ballots 1836-1892*. Baltimore: Johns Hopkins Press, 1955.

Carmer, Carl. *The Fishing Creek Confederacy*. New York, NY: David McKay Co., 1955.

Columbia and Montour Counties., vols. I and II. Chicago: J. H. Beers and Company, 1915.

Dabney, R. L., DD. *A Defense of Virginia (and Through Her, of the South)*. Harrisonburg, Virginia: Sprinkle Publications, 1977.

Democratic Party of Pennsylvania. *Proceedings of the Nob Mountain Meeting*. Philadelphia: McLaughlin Brothers, 1865.

Evans, Rachel P. *History of Fishingcreek Valley*. Orangeville, PA: Kline, 1939.

Freeze, John G. *A History of Columbia County, Pennsylvania.* Bloomsburg, Pennsylvania: Elwell and Bittenbender, 1883.

Godcharles, Frederick A. *Pennsylvania; Political, Governmental, Military and Civil.* New York: American Historical Society, 1933.

Gosse, John. *A History of Columbia County from the Earliest Times.* Bloomsburg, Pennsylvania: Elwell and Bittenbender, 1883.

Historical and Biographical Annals of Columbia and Montour Counties, Pennsylvania. Chicago: J.H. Beers and Co., 1915

Hummel, William W. "The Military Occupation of Columbia County." *Pennsylvania Magazine of History and Biography,* July 1956, 320-338.

Hummel, William. *Charles Buckalew: Democratic Statesman in a Republican Era.* University of Pittsburgh, 1963.

Marshall, John A. *The American Bastille.* Philadelphia: Evans, Stoddart and Company, 1870.

McClure, Alexander K. *Old Time Notes of Pennsylvania,* volume II. Philadelphia: The John C. Winston Co., 1905.

McHenry, Mary. *Military Invasion of Columbia County.* WPA Transcript Project No. 15253, 1930.

Robinson, Edgar E. *The Presidential Vote, 1896-1932.* Stanford, California: Stanford University Press, 1934.

Scammon, Richard M. *America at the Polls.* Pittsburgh: University of Pittsburgh Press, 1965.

Schnure, William M. "The Fishing Creek Confederacy." Report to the Northumberland County Historical Society, Vol. XVIII, November 1, 1950. Valley View, Pennsylvania: The Valley View Citizen, 1951.

Sherman, Barbara. "Fishing Creek Confederacy: Fact and Fiction." August 14, 1951. (pamphlet).

Turner, George A. *Civil War Letters from Soldiers and Civilians of Columbia County, Pennsylvania.* New York, NY: American Heritage, Custom Publishing, 1996.

Turner, George A. "Civil War Dissent in Columbia County, Pennsylvania." *Carver Journal* 9 (1991): 43-59.

US Congress. Senate. Biographical Directory of the American Congress. S. Doc., 92nd Congress, 1st session, 1971.

Walker, G.H. and C.F. Jewett. *Atlas of Columbia and Montour Counties.* New York, NY: F.W. Beers and Co., 1876.

Newspapers

Bloomsburg Enterprise. December 28, 2008.

Bloomsburg Republican. September 9, 1864.

Columbia County Democrat. October 1 and 22, 1864.

Morning Press. [Bloomsburg] July 2, 1969; July 23, 1969; February 15, 1982; February 22, 1982.

Philadelphia Bulletin. September 7, 1864.

Philadelphia Inquirer. September 6-7, 1864; October 26, 1864.

Philadelphia Inquirer Magazine. May 6, 1863.

Press Enterprise. [Bloomsburg] October 1987 and February 24, 2003.

Sunbury American. August 20, 1864.

Sunbury Gazette. August 20, September 10, 1864.

Wilkes-Barre Independent. March 9, 1924.

Wilkes-Barre Times. September 25, 1991.

Internet Sources

"Fishing Creek Confederacy." www.bentonnews.net/features/applemanindex.htm.

"The Writings of Senator Charles Buckalew." www.mtholyoke.edu/acad/polit/damy/articles/buckalew.htm.

www.bentonnews.net/features/Appleman.htm.

http://en.wikipedia.org/wiki/Columbia_County,_Pennsylvania www.uselectionatlas.org